PRAISE FOR

KRISTINE KATHRYN RUSCH

"Rusch is a great storyteller."

—*RT Book Reviews*

"Whether [Rusch] writes high fantasy, horror, sf, or contemporary fantasy, I've always been fascinated by her ability to tell a story with that enviable gift of invisible prose. She's one of those very few writers whose style takes me right into the story—the words and pages disappear as the characters and their story swallows me whole....Rusch has style."

—Charles de Lint

"A masterful writer is at work."

—Orson Scott Card

"Rusch's greatest strength...is her ability to close down a story and leave the reader feeling that the author could not possibly have wrung any more satisfaction out of the piece."

—*The Kansas City Star*

"Rusch is a great storyteller—easily the equal of Patterson or Koontz."

—*Analog*

"Kristine Kathryn Rusch is one of the best writers in the field."

—*SFRevu*

"[Rusch's] writing style is simple but elegant, and her characterization excellent."

—Mark Morris
Beyond

"Kristine Kathryn Rusch's crime stories are exceptional, both in plot and in style."

—Ed Gorman
Mystery Scene Magazines

PRAISE FOR THE RETRIEVAL ARTIST SERIES

"If you love puzzle mysteries, crime novels, well-invented sci-fi worlds, or stories about characters you can believe in and care about, you owe it to yourself to give Rusch's Retrieval Artist novels a try."

—Orson Scott Card
New York Times bestselling author

"What links [Miles Flint] to his most memorable literary ancestors is his hard-won ability to perceive the complex nature of morality and live with the burden of his own inevitable failure."

—*Locus*

PRAISE FOR THE SMOKEY DALTON SERIES
(WRITING AS KRIS NELSCOTT)

"Nelscott's series setting, in the turbulent late '60s, gives her books layers of issues of racism, class, and war, all of which still seem to remain sadly timely today."
—Oregonian

"Nelscott has her own, very distinct voice, and her series creates its own deeply satisfying pleasures and cogent points."
—Seattle Times

"Nelscott is good at conveying the edgy caution that blacks once brought to their movements among white society."
—Houston Chronicle

"(A) crime writer deliberately taking chances."
—Chicago Tribune

"It's not hard to draw parallels between Nelscott's PI Smokey Dalton and Walter Mosley's Easy Rawlins, another secretive, canny black man trying to solve mysteries while circumspectly navigating the white world. But Dalton's no knock-off. (Would you label the hundreds of hard-boiled detectives who've appeared in Raymond Chandler's wake mere Marlow Xeroxes because they're white?)"
—Entertainment Weekly

Also by
Kristine Kathryn Rusch

The Retrieval Artist Series:

The Disappeared
Extremes
Consequences
Buried Deep
Paloma
Recovery Man
Duplicate Effort
Anniversary Day
Blowback

The Smokey Dalton Series (as Kris Nelscott):

A Dangerous Road
Smoke-Filled Rooms
Thin Walls
Stone Cribs
War at Home
Days of Rage

Five Diverse Detectives

Kristine Kathryn Rusch

wMG
Publishing

Five Diverse Detectives

"Blind," by Kristine Kathryn Rusch was first published in *Alien Abductions*, edited by Martin H. Greenberg and John Helfers, Daw Books, October, 1999.

"Discovery," by Kristine Kathryn Rusch was first published in *Alfred Hitchcock's Mystery Magazine*, November, 2008.

"Stomping Mad" by Kristine Kathryn Rusch was first published in *Return of the Dinosaurs,* edited by Mike Resnick and Martin H. Greenberg, Daw Books, 1997.

"Dragon Slayer" by Kristine Kathryn Rusch was first published in German as "Ein Fall für Rumaad," *Feueratem: Das Grosse Drachen-Lesebuch*, edited by Michael Nagula, Knaur, 2003.

"The Retrieval Artist" by Kristine Kathryn Rusch was first published in *Analog SF*, June, 2000.

WMG PUBLISHING
www.wmgpublishing.com

Contents

Five Diverse Detectives

Kristine Kathryn Rusch

Introduction

I READ EVERYTHING. I had no idea what genre was until I was in college and my creative writing class buddy, Kevin J. Anderson, explained genre to me. He was horrified that I had no idea that books had categories. I simply figured those little rocket stickers that the library attached to the Andre Norton books I read were there to help me find more books like Andre Norton's. I had no idea that the rockets signified science fiction, any more than I realized that the first short story I handed into my creative writing class was "fantasy in the *Twilight Zone* mode." But Kevin knew. And he taught me.

Or tried to. Kev, now a bestselling author, still shakes his head at my genre mishaps. Most of those mishaps occur in my brain. Try as I might, I can't limit myself to one genre. I write under several pen names, including Kris Nelscott (1960s noir mysteries) and Kristine Grayson (paranormal romance/urban fantasy).

The biggest problem—for me and my editors—is that I write in more than one genre *in the same story*. Some editors

1

love that. Some hate it. The sales force at book publishers really hate it. What am I writing? Science fiction? Mystery? (But, folks, I'm writing science fiction *and* mystery.)

Sometimes the world catches up to me. Paranormal romance didn't really exist when I started my writing career. The Gothic novel, which combined ghosts and contemporary romance or horror and contemporary romance (so long as the horror was "suggested" and not overt), had died a spectacular death. (Lately it's been revived.) Mystery editors claimed mystery readers did not like anything "out of the ordinary." (Clearly mystery editors of that time hadn't talked to a lot of mystery readers.) Science fiction readers didn't want "romantic crap" spoiling their serious novels.

But slowly, these things changed. Fortunately for me. Short fiction editors have always given my wayward imagination a home. *Ellery Queen's Mystery Magazine* has published everything from straight mysteries by me to mystery/science fiction. *Asimov's Science Fiction Magazine* has published everything from straight science fiction to science fiction mysteries. (Yes, apparently there is a difference.) I just mail the stories, hoping they'll find a home. And more often than not, they do. Even the cross-genre ones.

In this short collection, you'll find a variety of genres along with the diverse detectives. Don't worry. All of the stories here are mysteries, and all of them have crimes that get solved. But the detectives range from a Secret Master of Science Fiction fandom to an actual dragon. There is a "normal" detective—the guy who sits in his office and waits for the gorgeous woman to walk in—but he works on the Moon. The lawyer and the crash site detective seem relatively plain by comparison.

The collection begins with the crash-site detective. "Blind" is set in Seavy Village, a fictional town on the Oregon Coast, where strange things happen. I've written straight mysteries set in Seavy Village, horror novels, dark fantastic short stories, and science fiction. You won't know which genre I tacked onto the detective story until the end of this one, so enjoy.

"Discovery" is set in New Mexico. I had no idea Pita Cardenas even was a detective until she got nominated for a Shamus Award, given to the best detective story written in a given year. This story is one of two straightforward mystery stories in this volume. Nothing supernatural or fantastic here.

There isn't anything supernatural or fantastic in "Stomping Mad" either, but it feels like there should be. "Stomping Mad" first appeared in a science fiction/fantasy anthology about dinosaurs. The dinosaurs in this story are of the convention-going type. "Stomping Mad" is set at Dinocon, a made-up science fiction convention. The story marks the first appearance of Spade, who solves crimes at sf conventions. Spade has made other appearances, mostly in *Alfred Hitchcock's Mystery Magazine*. He's not all that conventional (pun intended) either.

From dinosaurs (of the fake variety) to dragons of the real variety. Rumaad is a reluctant detective, but he discovers a heinous crime and feels compelled to solve it. The world here is not ours (do we have dragons solve mysteries?), but the story itself is pure mystery.

Just like the detective in "The Retrieval Artist" is classic: a man who works alone and handles difficult cases from his shabby office. That his office happens to be on the Moon does make him different, as well as the fact that he calls himself a Retrieval Artist instead of a detective, but Miles Flint is in the Raymond Chandler mode. Flint has gone on to star in nine novels to date, which *io9* calls one of the top ten sf/detective series ever written. This story, his first appearance but chronologically late in his career, was nominated for science fiction's prestigious Hugo award.

So five stories, four human detectives, one classic detective, three stories set in the here and now, one set on the Moon, and one set in a fantastic land we can't see out of our windows. No matter how hard I try, I can't stick to one genre. And since you picked up this collection, I hope that means you can't either.

Enjoy!

—*Kristine Kathryn Rusch*
Lincoln City, Oregon
January 3, 2011

Blind

FELTON WOODS, outside the small coastal town of Seavy Village, Oregon, has a certain place in my memory. Whenever I think of it, I think of a particular moonlit evening when my brother Richard and I decided to dare the ghosts.

It was 1974. Richard was twelve. I was ten and small for my age. Usually, he thought of me as the annoying younger brother, but that night, he needed me. He had bragged to his buddies that he always went to Felton Woods on the nights of a full moon, and they hadn't believed him. So, as proof, he promised a Polaroid, taken near the fairy circle, with the moonlight shining all around and the pocket-knife he always carried on a rock in the center of the circle.

Richard had lied, of course. In those days, Richard usually lied to puff himself up. Later, as an adult, I learned that such behavior was a sign of insecurity, but then I simply saw it as part of Richard. And I usually got dragged into the lies when he needed help proving he had actually been telling the truth.

I was a little enabler, and was just beginning to realize it.

The night of the full moon was a school night. The next day was the annual spelling bee—something I was good at that my brother was not—and I wanted to have a good night sleep. When Richard shook me awake, leaning across my bottom bunk to find me pressed up against the wall, I mumbled, "Don wanna," so many times that he climbed on the bunk and sat on me. We tussled silently in the dark so that we wouldn't wake our parents in the room next door, and finally Richard pinned my arms against my race car pillow cases.

"Give?" he whispered.

"No," I said, and tried to buck him off.

"I need your help, Scott," he said, and that got me to stop moving. He'd never asked for my help before.

"Yeah?" I said.

"Yeah." He got off the bed and threw clothes at me. I put them on. Then we snuck into the kitchen, got Dad's utility flashlight, and the new Polaroid, and tiptoed out the back door.

Our house was on a small hill that had an ocean view on one side and a view of Felton woods on the other. The moon was so bright that it seemed like Mom had left the porch light on. I could see Richard's shadow. I followed him across the yard, under the clothesline, and to the deer path that my father kept trying to block with fallen tree limbs and bags of clipped grass from our mower. Richard and I walked around the mass of limbs and grass, which, that late in the fall, had begun to smell ripe.

The path was narrow and steep and somewhere along it, I clutched small branches for support. A hawk swooped past us that night, and we heard an owl in the distance. I wasn't frightened, just surprised at the brightness of the moonlight and angry at Richard's assumption that I would do anything if he asked, no matter how stupid. The fact that the assumption was correct somehow made it worse.

I think Richard was scared, though. He went first and moved slowly, using that flashlight's beam as if it were a raygun that could zap anything in our path. His breathing was harsh and ragged, and more than once, he squealed softly as some creature darted through the grass. For the first time that I knew of, he had trapped himself well and good, and I probably would have remembered that night for the rest of my life for simply that reason. But as it were, other things made the night just as memorable.

The fairy circle in Felton Woods was really just a clearing where no trees grew. What looked like the remains of an out-of-control campfire had left a dirt circle wide enough to fit four or five tents. In the center of that circle was a flat-topped boulder that looked as if it had grown, mushroom-like, from the blackness of the earth. In the middle of the day, sunlight streamed into the circle, illuminating the rock as if someone in heaven had placed a spotlight on its dark surface. The trees diffused the light everywhere else in the wood.

As we approached the fairy circle, we could hear the burble of Felton Creek. In the winter, the creek grew too wide and deep to cross, and sometimes it flooded the lower part of the wood. In the summer, the creek was little more than a trickle—and sometimes, in dry years, not even that. I didn't think I had ever been to the woods when the creek lived up to its name, and gurgled through its banks just like it was supposed to.

I was getting cold and tired and thirsty, and I knew, somehow, that Mrs. Yates had chosen Czechoslovakia as one of the place names we had to identify and spell. I always misplaced the "l" in that word, and as I walked, I tried to remember if it was C-z-e-c-h-l or C-z-e-c-h-o-l or—

Richard stuck out his bony arm to stop me, and I slammed right into it. "Hey!"

"Shh," he whispered, putting a finger to his lips in case I didn't get the message.

There was a sound over the burbling, a light wail, almost like the wind blowing through a poorly sealed window. I felt the hair rise on the back of my neck, and it took all of my strength not to grab Richard's arm.

Instead, I pushed it away and kept going down the path.

"Scott!" he whispered. "Scotty!"

My heart was beating too hard, and my throat had gone dry, but I continued walking. Part of my defiance came from my anger at Richard, and part of it came from my desire to get back home to bed. But the largest part was that no sound, wailing or not, would get the better of me.

I could see clearly without the flashlight. The moon sent a silvery glow over the entire meadow. The rock in the center of the dirt circle shone as if someone had painted it with reflecting paint.

The wail had stopped.

"Give me your damn knife," I said, not bothering to whisper. Richard didn't seem to notice, nor did he seem to care that I had used a forbidden word. Instead he scrambled the rest of the way down the path, and handed me the knife.

I walked into the dirt circle and put the knife in the center of the boulder. The rock's flat surface wasn't flat up close. It had ripples, like chocolate frosting that had dried with the spatula marks still in it. I balanced the knife between the grooves, where its silver and pearl handle caught the moonlight, and then I walked out of the circle. I grabbed the Polaroid from Richard, brought the whole thing to my face, and found the knife through the view-finder. The knife looked thin, insubstantial. I was too far away. Without moving the camera, I walked closer, until the knife was in the center of the frame.

Then I pressed the big red "shoot" button, and listened to the camera hum and whir as it processed the film. I hit the button twice more before taking the undeveloped pictures that had fallen to the ground and thrusting the camera back at Richard.

"There," I said. "We're done."

He wasn't looking at me. He was looking at his knife. It was lost in a shroud of ground fog which I could have sworn hadn't been there a moment before. The fog was shaped like a human being, bent over to examine the surface of the rock.

The sight took my breath away, but only for a moment. The air was getting chillier. Ground fog was always bad near water, and would get worse as a night progressed.

I didn't want to go up that path blind.

I walked back into the circle, and reached through the fog. The knife was higher than I had expected it to be. And colder. It dropped into my palm, and as it did, the ground fog rose, like a person standing up. I yelped, then backed up. My fingers closed around the knife, and I remembered to thrust it into my pocket, before I started to run.

Richard was already up the hill ahead of me. His feet had dug long holes in the path's dirt where he had slipped and slid as he hurried his way to the top. He was leaning against Mother's clothes pole, taking deep shuddery breaths. In his hand, he clutched the Polaroids, and the camera hung around his neck.

"Jerkwad," I said to him when I could breathe. "You left me down there."

"You shouldn't've gone back in that circle."

"Someone had to get your dumb knife." I pulled it out of my pocket and tossed it to the ground beside him. "Don't ask me to do anything again."

And then I stomped into the house, climbed back in bed, and shivered for the next hour. I fell asleep thinking how the fog had felt like fingertips brushing against my skin as the knife fell into my palm.

The next morning I misspelled Czechoslovakia, and was eliminated on the second round. I didn't know that Richard and the Polaroids were creating quite a stir among the sixth grade boys. I didn't know that a father of one of the boys specialized in paranormal research, and thought the photos were something special. I didn't know that he would write an article about our experiences in the woods—without talking to me—and would get us grounded for a month for a) going out at night alone and b) stealing the camera. I also didn't know that those photographs would haunt me for the rest of my life.

You see, on the photographs themselves, the ground fog appeared in its strangely human shape. It looked as if it were contemplating us, then as if it were interested in the knife. It appeared to reach out a clearly defined hand in the last photo, as if it were going to pick up the knife.

The *Skeptical Inquirer,* years later, agreed with me: what we had seen was ground fog. Other debunkers claimed everything from flawed film to poor photography (one even suggested that I had a thumb over part of the lens). None of which I tried to deny, although Richard did. I wanted no part of any of it.

But the believers had one frightened little boy—who grew up into a frightened man—on their side. They also had a bit of strange ground fog that didn't show up on the dirt around the boulder, only in that long thin strangely human column. They also had the stories about Felton Wood, which included strange disappearances, unexplained noises, and the inability for anything to grow in the circle where we had put the knife.

It all made for a great spook story, and if I had been inclined to believe in spooks, I might have let that memory of the chill, dank fog fingers against my palm convince me too. But since then I'd been in fog a hundred times, and sometimes it felt like little needles pricking my skin, and sometimes it felt like hands caressing my face, and sometimes it felt like cold damp air giving me chills.

I believe in nothing, but remain open to everything. Only I need more proof than a quick touch against the palm, a knife that felt as if it were dropped instead of picked up, and Polaroids of something that could be a ghost or could be ground fog or could be a flaw in film.

So, except for the occasional interviewer who would dig me up for a retelling of my experience, I didn't think about Felton Woods. At least, not until my brother died, and I found myself there one final time.

***

My brother Richard was the kind of man who succeeded young and allowed everything to go downhill from there. He was the star quarterback for the Seavy High Sailors, but his talents didn't extend beyond our small town. He married the homecoming queen, just like he was supposed to, but after high school, they both looked a little lost. He flunked out of Oregon Coast Community College, and she never went, pregnant at the time with the first of their three daughters. He got a job managing a store, and that became his career. When my parents died in a car crash on Highway 20, hit head-on by a tourist trying to pass in a no-passing zone, Richard asked me if he could move into their house instead of selling it. He didn't want to pay rent.

I had no objections. I had gone to MIT on a National Merit Scholarship, and had discovered the great world beyond the Oregon Coast. Until my parents' funeral, I hadn't been back. I saw no reason to spend my life in a town that couldn't pass a referendum to expand their two-room library.

My degree got me into computers back when you had to learn a second language to do so. I joined up with Microsoft when it was still a young company, and through its generous stock program, I became one of Seattle's many Microsoft millionaires. I never purchased additional stock past what the company allowed, and I used my dividends to buy into other companies. I retired at the age of thirty-two to manage my portfolio, and to see the world. By the time I returned home to attend my parents' funeral, I had already been to all seven continents, and I had just found my new avocation.

I became a historic crash site detective.

It started as a lark. I joined some friends of mine from MIT on a trip into the Mojave. They were looking for metal left by the crash of an experimental aircraft in 1958. They had used historic documents, some obtained through the Freedom of Information Act, to determine where the craft went down. They needed people to help them comb several square miles of desert, looking for bits of metal left to deteriorate in the sun.

I was the one who found the first piece. I saw it glinting beneath a bit of sagebrush. The metal was a shard of aluminum no bigger than a quarter, with the telltale green of aviation zinc chromate paint on one side.

From that moment, I was hooked. I went on subsequent trips, and soon became the coordinator for several more, since I was the man who had no nine-to-five job. We were all amateurs, and we all loved the work. Even after aviation historians began to take note of us, we still refused payment for the research. We were all very aware of the fact that our work came out of tragedy. We couldn't work modern crash sites—we were all too squeamish and would, I think, have been out of our depths—so we felt as if we were resurrecting the memories of men who had died long ago, in courageous ways.

Of course, along the way, we found things we couldn't identify. A scrap of metal near Barstow that could be crumpled and then would return to its own shape as if it had been ironed; a slip of paper that hadn't deteriorated over time, with the tensile strength equal to that of steel; and a bit of something that looked like a child's hair ribbon, that appeared pink to some of us, gold to others, and which shared some of the same color properties as an oil slick. Most of these we gave to colleagues in related industries, and we never saw them again. But sometimes, as with the items listed above, I kept the oddities, and put them in a safety deposit box, just so that I could remind myself there were things in the universe that human beings couldn't yet explain.

One of the things human beings couldn't explain was exactly how my brother Richard died. He was found near Felton Creek, a victim of exposure.

His wife had called me the day he was found. The conversation had been a strange one; she hadn't been crying, but I could hear tears in her voice. Behind her, other voices spoke softly, and I knew that her family had already rallied around her and the girls. They didn't need me, but she had almost begged me to come.

Perhaps she had been afraid that I wouldn't go to Seavy Village for my brother's funeral, even though I was only seven hours away by car. After all, I had told them repeatedly that I didn't plan to come back, and all our visits were on my dime in places around the world that I had chosen to broaden my nieces' horizons, to show them that there was more to life than a tourist town with only seven thousand permanent residents.

Or perhaps she had spoken to everyone that way, from me to the owner of the outlet franchise store that Richard managed. I had no way of telling, and I didn't really ponder the information. Not at first. When your older brother dies mysteriously and unexpectedly at the age of 37, you spend all of your time trying to accept the world without him. Even though I saw Richard as something of a failure, as a man who never reached his full potential, I also knew him as my older brother, as a constant so fine that life without him seemed like suddenly discovering that the sun was going to rise in the west for the rest of my life. It wasn't possible that I could continue without Richard, that one day I would be 37, and he would never get past that age. I thought we had time. To learn that we didn't, and that we never would have, consumed me so that I didn't even notice the drive.

Nor did I note that Seavy Village had gotten bigger, until I reached the outskirts of town and found houses there, dozens of them, new developments built up around what had once been a fairly ugly and poorly maintained 9-hole golf course. Now the course was part of a fitness center, and it boasted 18 beautiful holes. The houses, according to a sign, sold for $200,000 each, and all had views of either the mountains or the ocean.

The stores had changed, but they always did that, even when I was a boy. A modern library stood in what used to be the old city center, and across the street from it was the factory outlet mall where Richard had worked. Beside that was a six-plex movie theater, and several newly built hotels. Seavy Village no longer deserved its "village" moniker. It was a healthy and growing town.

The road to the house was the same. The state hadn't widened 101 yet—not that they could without damaging prime real estate (there is only so much land between the ocean and the mountains)—and so, even though the buildings were different, the twists and turns of the place where I had learned how to drive remained the same. I turned onto the side road that led away from the ocean to what had been my parents' house. When we were growing up, the small turquoise blue ranch-style building had been the only one on the ridgeline. Now there were houses on either side of the ridge, and down the road as far as I could see.

When I pulled up in front of the house, I had to park on the lawn. Half a dozen cars filled the wide driveway, and four more were also on the stretch of grass that had once held my mother's clotheslines. My youngest niece, Stacy, sat on a barstool inside the garage. She clutched a basketball in both hands. Her blond hair fell across her face, and for a moment, she looked like her mother had at the same age, pensive and pretty. Then she brought her head up, and I saw the blending of Richard in her face, the soft features that made her uniquely Stacy.

I got out of the car. She didn't smile at me. Instead, she dropped the basketball, ran across the driveway, and flung herself in my arms.

She was almost as tall as I was, and the impact of her thin body nearly knocked me over. She clung tightly and I held her back, realizing, for the first time, how much I needed this closeness as well. After Cindy's call, I had just gotten into the car and drove. I hadn't even told friends where I was going.

Finally, Stacy broke away. Her eyes were swollen from crying, and her cheeks looked chapped. With one hand, she tucked loose hair behind her ears.

"Don't believe them, Uncle Scott," she said. "They're all lying."

Whatever I had expected her to say, it wasn't that. "Who's lying?" I asked.

"Everyone." She bit her lower lip, scraping off the chapped skin with her teeth. Blood appeared on the side of her mouth, and I realized she'd been doing this since her father died. If she didn't quit soon, she'd rub her mouth raw. "They say Daddy left Mommy, but he didn't. I was with him that last night. He didn't plan to go anywhere."

I felt as if I were playing catch up. I touched the corner of her mouth. "You're hurting yourself, honey."

She jerked away as if I had burned her. "You don't be-lieve me either."

"I didn't say that." I frowned. "It's just I don't know what happened to your dad, except that he was found dead."

"He was gone for a week, and then they found him in Felton Woods," she said.

"Was he murdered?"

She shook her head. "You know how he always had crazy schemes. They said this one just went wrong."

Crazy schemes, yes. But my brother never acted on the schemes, not as he grew older. Not after that little in-cident with the Polaroids and the knife in the fairy circle.

"What was the scheme?" I asked.

"I don't know!" her voice rose. "It wasn't like Dad. He never did anything dangerous. He wouldn't even let us go on those whale watching tours because he was afraid something would happen."

Just like our father. He had protected himself only to be killed on a routine drive, not an hour away from home.

I put my arm around her waist. "Let's go in, Stace, and see what's going on."

"You're not going to like it," she said. "I don't." But she came with me anyway.

The interior of the house smelled of dirty dishes, un-washed clothing, and casseroles thick with hamburger and American cheese. Voices came from the kitchen. I walked through the hallway decorated with school photographs, and into the living room. The large double-paned picture window with a view of the ocean remained the same as did the room's general contours. Otherwise it was unfamiliar. The furniture was old and faded, the couch shrouded in a green coverlet designed to hide furniture that needed upholstering. Richard and Cindy's wedding picture hung over the fireplace, and a large mirror hung over the couch, making the small room seem somehow smaller.

A dozen people stood in the center, talking, surrounding Cindy. She had put on weight since I last saw her, and her eyes were puffy as well. In her right hand she held a tattered box of Kleenex, and in her left, a stuffed dog that appeared new. The people around her had familiar faces, and some of them I recognized from Richard and Cindy's wedding almost twenty years before. My oldest niece, Heather, was leaning against the built-in bookshelf on the far wall, watching everyone. The middle niece, April, was nowhere to be seen.

Stacy came in the room behind me. Heather noticed me at that moment, but didn't leave her post.

"Mother," Stacy said. "Uncle Scott is here."

Cindy turned then, and came toward me, arms out. I let her hug me, but somehow I didn't need this hug like I had needed Stacy's. Stacy's had felt mutual. Cindy's felt as if she were trying to draw something from me, something I did not have to give.

As she pulled back, she held my upper arms in a visegrip. "Oh, Scotty," she said. "At last."

I made myself smile, felt how insincere it was, how much even that small movement hurt. "I came as soon as you called."

She nodded as if she hadn't really heard me. "Now we can ask you," she said, and she turned to the others as if she were speaking for all of them. "What was Richard doing that last week? Why did he go see you?"

Her fingers bit into my biceps. I would have bruises in the morning. "He didn't come to see me, Cindy."

"Yes," she said. "Yes, he did."

I shook my head. Heather was staring at me, her pretty brown eyes dull. Stacy stood close to me as if she were protecting me.

"Come on, son," said Cindy's father. He had grown shorter in the intervening years. "No need to cover for Richard now."

"I'm not," I said. "The last time I saw him, Cindy, was in London. With you."

She was shaking her head, her eyes closed. This was clearly not what she wanted to hear. She let go of my arms.

"There's no need to lie, Scott," Cindy's mother said.

"I know," I said. "I'm not lying."

The room was silent. Everyone was watching me. Stacy slipped one slim hand in mine.

"Does someone want to tell me what happened here?" I asked. "Or should I leave?"

"No." Cindy took a deep shuddery breath and pulled herself together visibly. In that movement, I saw the remains of the slender girl who had managed, every halftime, to do a double twist ending in splits, even though the entire maneuver terrified her. "I'll tell you."

And so she did.

IT ALL STARTED when one of the producers for a cable television program called *American's Strangest Stories* contacted Richard about our night in Felton Woods. Felton Woods was making the national UFO websites because of all the strange disappearances that were taking place there. Dogs had vanished off leashes, children had gone missing, and adults also disappeared, all after saying they were going to Felton Woods. People claimed they saw the dogs disappear, but no one had actually seen the children or adults disappear.

Most of the people who had disappeared were tourists, and most of them had severe family problems. All of the children were involved in some sort of parental custody dispute. Local authorities seemed to think these things important; in all cases, the police found explanations other than mysterious events in the woods. No bodies were ever found.

When the producer came to visit, she was young, beautiful, and very businesslike. When she saw the battered Polaroids, and heard Richard's story, she had smiled at him condescendingly and asked if he had been to the woods lately. When he said he hadn't, she had thanked him for his time, offered him $250 for the use of the Polaroids on the show, and promised that she would call him for "deep background."

The show aired in April. She used the Polaroids, but never called him. His name wasn't even mentioned.

But the show had aired with the promise of a follow-up in the fall. Richard became obsessed with being part of that follow-up. It was all he could talk about. He felt that the phenomenon of Felton Woods had started with him— and here Cindy had bowed her head, then shrugged. "I'm sure he meant both of you," she had said—and he was determined to be sure he was still a part of it all.

And then Heather broke into the tale.

"He stopped coming home at night," she said. "Or if he came home, he would leave again."

"Usually with a flashlight," Stacy said from beside me.

Heather shot her a how-stupid-can-you-be? look. "He was seeing someone."

"He was going to the woods," Stacy said.

Heather shook her head.

"It doesn't matter," Cindy said. "What matters is that he disappeared a week before he died. He led me to believe he was going to see you, Scott, to see if you remembered anything else about that night."

I sighed. "He didn't even call."

"He had a girlfriend," Heather said.

"Did not," Stacy said.

"Girls." Cindy sounded tired. "I guess now we'll never know."

My brother could have had a girlfriend. He had been tempted once before, after our parents died, but he had been afraid of what an affair would do to his family. He and I spent many a late night on the phone, on my dime, while he discussed the lack of direction in his life.

He hadn't called this time.

"I don't understand," I said. "If you thought he was with me, how do you explain his death in Felton Woods?"

"Maybe you concocted a scheme, helped him like you used to, so the producer would come back. Maybe he did it wrong, or maybe he started without you, or…" Cindy's voice trailed off. Apparently I had been her last hope. Apparently she had convinced herself this silly story of hers was true, and she used it to prevent herself from seeing what seemed plain to her parents and the rest of her family.

But the whole thing seemed odd, and so did Cindy. At the time I attributed her behavior to grief. Later I would remember she had shown signs of it on our last visit, in London, six months before. A willingness to believe the strangest things. Accusations when no crime had been committed. The belief that Richard and I were somehow concocting schemes without her.

"Daddy couldn't have been having an affair," Stacy said. "I was with him that last night."

"You couldn't have been," Heather said. "You were too sick."

"I snuck out."

Heather shook her head. "You don't have to lie for him."

"I'm *not*."

"Girls," Cindy said tiredly. She ran a hand through her limp hair. Everyone watched her. "Do you need a place to stay, Scott?"

The offer was half-hearted. She didn't want anyone else in her place, particularly the man who had blown her comfortable scenario all to hell.

"I reserved a room down at the Lodge," I said, even though I hadn't. Money talked. I would find some place to take me, no matter how full the town was.

She nodded. Her mother sat down beside her on the couch. "The funeral's tomorrow," her father said. "Viewing's tonight." And with those few words, I had been dismissed.

***

STACY ACCOMPANIED ME OUTSIDE. She was still holding my hand. "I want you to stay here, Uncle Scott."

"Your mom doesn't," I said. "Besides, you need your privacy."

She shook her head. "We need someone sane. April won't come out of her room. Heather stomps around like it's our fault Dad's dead, and Mom won't stop crying."

That made me want to stay even less. "Look, sweetie," I said, "as soon as I have a room number, I'll call you with it. If things get too bad, come on down, and I'll play you a mean game of gin rummy."

Her grin was quick, but shallow. I hadn't touched her heart. "Uncle Scott?"

"Hmm?"

"If I gave you my dad's notes, would you read them?"

"His notes?"

She nodded. "He was trying to do something, like you. He thought if he could prove—well, his notes say it better."

I didn't answer her one way or another. What I was listening to was behind the words. "That visit with the producer really shook him up, didn't it?"

She bit her bottom lip again, then stopped when she saw me watching. "He said he was turning forty and had nothing to show for it."

Ouch, I thought. What a thing to say to your daughter.

"He said you were the one who did everything. You were the one with the courage. Even that night in the woods, you were the one who put the knife on the boulder, you were the one who photographed everything, and you were the one who got the knife back when Dad ran away."

He had never told that full story before, not to anyone. I hadn't contributed to his lie, but I hadn't corrected it either.

"He had a great family," I said, not to enable him any longer, but because I didn't like the hurt in her eyes when she spoke of his failure. "I've never been able to find that."

"We're your family, Uncle Scott," she said. And at that moment, I realized she was right. They were my family. The only family I had. And they were a mess.

What had you been doing these last few weeks, Richard? What was worth your sacrifice?

"Have you read his papers?" I asked.

She shook her head. "He made me promise not to. And I couldn't show them to Mom or April or Heather. But he didn't make me promise not to show them to you."

So she had doubts as well. She was protecting her father, and doubting him at the same time. When I left, he had a few years on his own, and then Stacy had arrived, another little enabler.

Maybe that had been the reason she and I were always so close. Neither of us could stand up to Richard when he needed someone to help him get his way.

"What happened that last night?" I asked. "You said you saw him in the woods."

She ran a hand through her hair, a gesture so like her mother's that it stopped my breath. "I had a migraine," she said, and then she flushed so red that it looked as if her skin were going to explode. "I've been getting them lately."

Puberty, I wanted to say. It didn't scare me like it did her, but it explained her new height and her gawky poise. I wanted to tell her that migraines were normal, that at least three of my girlfriends had suffered the same thing, but I remained silent.

"I went to bed without supper. I get nauseous sometimes too."

I nodded.

"I fell asleep, and when I woke up, there was moonlight coming in my window." Stacy's room was on the far end of the house. After Richard and Cindy had moved in, they had added two rooms on the narrow space left on the lot. They had planned to build a second story, but never had the funds. I didn't respond to their hints for a loan.

"Something about the moonlight made me think of Dad, and that producer, and the whole mess. I missed him." She looked behind me, at the trail to the woods. "So I went down to the fairy circle. He called my name. He was hiding in the bushes near the creek. I'd never heard him sound so scared."

"Was he all right?"

She nodded. "He had a tent and everything. He said he was waiting."

"For?"

"I don't know. But he said he'd be home as soon as he had proof. Then he told me to leave, said it wasn't safe to come into the woods alone. I knew that, but I wasn't thinking clear—the migraine, I guess—and besides, I wanted to see him. He walked me up the path, and hugged me." She swallowed hard. "And that was the last time I saw him."

I leaned against my car. "Why doesn't anyone believe you?"

A slight frown crossed her forehead. "There wasn't any tent when they found him, and the coroner says he might have been dead for a day or two. They say I dreamed the whole thing because I wanted my dad to come home. Mom said it wasn't possible for me to go down the hill, not after I'd taken one of her sleeping pills. But I slept, Uncle Scott, and then I woke up. I was woozy, but I was awake. I remember feeling cold and going down that path. I remember hugging him."

She sounded like she wanted to convince herself more than me, but I was willing to believe her, at least at this point. "Give me his papers," I said. "I'll see what I can find."

***

THE PAPERS FIT into my briefcase. Apparently Richard hadn't bought a computer yet, or if he had, he hadn't used it for this. Everything was on yellow legal pads, covered in his tight narrow handwriting. Looking at it as I stuffed it in the briefcase made my heartache. My brother had been in trouble, and for the first time in his life, he hadn't come to me.

I managed to get a room in the Lodge after all. It was the off season, and because I was feeling so low, I decided to go for luxurious. They had a two-room suite, complete with living room, a gas fireplace and Jacuzzi, all with an ocean view. I took it, and lit the fire as soon as I entered the room. Then I set the briefcase aside, ordered dinner from room service, and pulled back the curtains.

It had started to rain. Another storm was building over the ocean, its clouds diffuse and elongated, indicating even heavier ran to come. Fall on the coast was always dicey—my least favorite season. Winter was cold and sunny, but fall was filled with storm after storm, making it feel as if the entire world were going to drown, one raindrop at a time.

While I waited for the food, I settled in the armchair near the fireplace and removed the legal pads. Richard had enough sense to date them, and so I put them in order, oldest on top. He had written a sort of diary beginning years before, with the first of the strange disappearances. Sometimes the gaps between notations were as long as six months, sometimes the notations appeared hourly.

I started to read, pausing only to open the door when my dinner arrived. Hours later, I turned the last page in the final notebook, leaned my head against the chair and closed my eyes. I knew I'd have to follow my brother into the woods one final time, and this time, I liked the idea even less than I had when I was ten.

***

THE FUNERAL WAS A LONG, surprising affair. Richard had known the entire town, and some people had driven in from as far away as Portland to offer their respects. The minister gave a small eulogy, then opened the floor to anyone who felt like speaking. Most people did.

Cindy sat in the front row through it all, silent sometimes, sobbing at others. April sat beside her, a wisp of her former self. I wondered if she was eating—or if anyone had bothered to find out—and vowed to spend some time with her while I was in town. Heather kept a protective arm around her mother throughout the service, and Stacy leaned away from all of them, twisting a handkerchief in her right hand.

I sat one row back and startled several old ladies who had forgotten that Richard had a brother. I was slimmer than he had been, but we were balding in the same way, and most of them confused me for him, at least momentarily. I could see it in their eyes, the sudden surprise, covered quickly as they realized I was a relative.

After the funeral, everyone went to Richard's house. Someone had cleaned up the surface mess, although the bathrooms were still filthy and dust covered the book-shelves. No one seemed to notice but me and perhaps I did because my mother had been a stickler for cleanliness, and she was probably turning in her grave at the way Cindy kept house. When Cindy asked me, in hushed tones, if I minded that she and the girls remained in the family homestead, I offered to deed the place to her. The last thing I wanted was to make my brother's family homeless.

And then it was all over, leaving only the flotsam and jetsam of a life cut short. Cindy and I spent a day hunting for investments, not that there were many, and then we spent another figuring out how she would make ends meet. We came to no conclusions—she hadn't been able to hold a job for longer than six months since Stacy was born—and I felt as if I were more concerned about this than she was. Cindy spent part of our time together just staring at things as if she didn't see them. I was wondering if, in her mind's eye, she saw Richard instead.

I also took everyone out for meals, insisting that April come as well. She didn't say anything to me for the first two days after the funeral—I was beginning to think she couldn't talk at all—and then she screamed at me when I had, in her presence, suggested grief counseling to her mother. After that, April seemed a bit more like herself, but I was still worried.

Richard's entire family seemed lost without him.

I had always thought Richard a failure. I hadn't realized how successful he had been, and how that success had differed from mine. He bound people together. I achieved goals. Two different ways of living. He had hundreds of people at his funeral. I realized if I died suddenly, I would have only had a handful, and of that handful, most would have been Richard's family.

I wished I could tell him that. I wished I could apologize. But I had missed my chance, and for the first time, I felt as if I had let an opportunity slip by.

So I took care of his family as best I could, helped them pick up the pieces without treading on their grief. And then, when I felt I could do no more, I called my team.

***

THEY DIDN'T WANT TO COME. They thought I was on a wild goose chase, and perhaps I was. So, for the first time in our joint history, I offered to pay them. And instead of refusing, they took me up on it.

At that time, the team still had its original members: Marietta Walker, an archivist for NASA; Tony Dryser, an historian who taught at Annapolis; Peter Bartell, an aviation historian who taught at Northwestern; and Joseph Harwell, a professional photographer. What they all had in common, besides an interest in U.S. test flight history, was that they attended MIT at the same time I did. I had been a peripheral part of their group, but in those days I was more interested in the inner workings of computers than in the adventures men had when they tried new aircraft.

The team came to Seavy Village in one large sports utility vehicle, rented at the Portland International airport, and driven, so the other three said, by Dryser as if he were expecting to get take-off orders at any moment. I got them all suites in the Lodge, and they piled in, energetic and resourceful, excited about a paid vacation at the coast.

I had forgotten, in the week I had been here, how exuberance felt. The entire town seemed depressed by Richard's death. My friends' energy almost seemed wrong.

Marietta hugged me when she saw me. She was a tiny woman built like a basketball player—all legs and torso—who somehow didn't make it to full height. She was wearing a white cotton t-shirt that accented her tanned skin, and army fatigue pants. The others hung back. They weren't as certain how to handle grief. None of them had experienced a serious loss, and since they'd known me, I'd lost my entire nuclear family.

When Marietta let me go, I let them all into my suite, and had room service bring us coffee and a snack. Dryser sprawled lengthwise on the couch, his thin frame—so appropriate to the desert—seemed out of place here. His wrinkled skin looked as if it might hydrate in the rain and suddenly make him full-faced and jolly.

Bartell was still dressed like the professor he was, tweed suit and scuffed shoes, his thinning blond hair combed to one side. He would dress like that until we went into the field, where he would don t-shirts and khakis and transform himself into a man of adventure. Harwell always looked like a man of adventure. His dark hair hadn't had a good cut in years, and that morning he had forgotten to shave. Only he was dressed appropriately for the coast, wearing a red and gray checked flannel shirt, faded blue jeans, and waterproof boots.

Harwell stood in the window, watching the ocean. Marietta perched on the arm of the couch, watching me. Bartell perused the books on the built-in shelves. Judging them was his manner of listening.

"You know," Dryser said, "you don't have to pay us the fee. Just room and board."

"Speak for yourself, Tony," Harwell said. "I'm losing a week of work here that I can ill afford."

"Scott doesn't look good, Joseph," Dryser said.

"But I'm well enough not to be talked about in the third person," I said. "I told you I'd pay for this, and I will. It's something I want to do, not something we normally do."

"We're just not used to proceeding backwards," Marietta said.

"That's not it." Bartell turned away from the books. "This feels too much like UFO-ology, and we've always stayed away from that."

I nodded. "You don't have to—"

"We're here," Marietta said.

Dryser put his hands behind his head. "Look at it this way, Peter. We're not investigating UFOs. We're investigating a death. Scott's brother died here."

"Of exposure," Bartell said, but gently so as not to offend me.

"Yeah," Harwell said. "What do the cops say about that?"

"They say he was having an affair. They say he was supposed to meet the lady in Felton Woods and either

33

she didn't show or she did, and he fell asleep, dying in the cold. They also say he'd been there for a few days, but my niece claims she saw him—with a tent and gear—the night before his body was found."

"Whom do you believe?" Marietta asked.

I shrugged. "Today I believe Stacy. Ask me tomorrow and I might believe the police."

"So we're doing this for you," Harwell said.

"I guess. I have the feeling he wouldn't have been out there if not for me."

"How's that?" Bartell asked.

"You've got to read the notebooks," I said, and handed them to him.

***

THE NEXT MORNING, we went to Felton Woods. They looked smaller than I remembered. The trees were second growth, sometimes third, spindly things that bent in the wind. Leaves covered the ground, and several of the Doug firs looked sick. Felton Creek was high, past the burbling stage, and nearly to the flood stage. After two weeks of near solid rain, it couldn't be anything else.

The fairy circle was smaller too. I had thought it the size of a parking lot when actually only one car would have fit on it. The boulder was little more than a large rock. Only it looked odd. There were no other rocks near it, and no place it could have fallen from above. Someone or something had once moved it there.

The team stared at the dirt circle as if it were something dangerous. We were all in our rain gear, and we looked like something out of a 1950s horror movie—yellow slickers against wet, dark trees, and a rain-swept sky.

For a moment, no one seemed to know what to do. Then Marietta dug into her pack for the Geiger counter. Bartell walked down to the creek, careful to hold tree branches in case he lost his footing. Harwell began taking pictures. Dryser was watching me.

I was having second thoughts. Marietta was right. We were proceeding backwards. Normally, we picked a test flight that ended in tragedy—the pilot dead, the experimental plane destroyed—and we searched until we found pieces of it. Sometimes we found enough to reassemble the plane. Sometimes all we did was locate the crash site for the pilot's families. Those were the tough cases, watching full adults sob as they remembered the night their father never came home, as they realized, perhaps for the first time, that he never would.

Here we had a mysterious site and strange evidence that my brother believed pointed to a UFO. The circle was not maintained by the park. In fact, I could remember a campaign in the mid-seventies to attempt to grow grass in that space. It hadn't worked. My brother added that, the mysterious disappearances, and strange lights that sometimes flashed over the ocean and came up with UFOs. Dryser, when he finished reading the tablets, came up with a sigh. "Sounds like people should stay out of Felton Woods."

Marietta had closed her eyes after her reading. Bartell had agreed with the cops. "You'll probably find all kinds of drug paraphernalia there. Evidence of some kind of illegal nightlife in that place."

Only Harwell had said nothing. He asked me a bunch of questions about the Polaroids, and then he had asked to see the pictures. I had given them to him and he had stared at them for a very long time.

Marietta's Geiger counter clicked as she held the wand over the dirt circle. "Radiation," she said softly. "Very low levels."

"Christ," I said. "Is it dangerous?"

"It's always dangerous, old bean," Dryser said. "But if you're expecting sudden outbreaks of strange cancers, you've got the wrong idea."

"It's localized," she said. "It doesn't leave the circle. It doesn't even go down to the stream."

"Creek," I said automatically.

"Creek," she repeated. Bartell had come up from the creek side. He had heard the entire exchange.

"How long has this circle been here?" he asked.

"According to my brother, since the fifties."

"Not good enough," Bartell said. "We need to pinpoint when."

"And how do you propose we do that?" I asked. "This town has only had a library for the past ten years. Not even the high school had one when I was a kid."

"Jesus," Harwell said. "How did you study?"

"There was a bookstore down the hill that had a reference area. The owner let kids use it."

"You've got to be kidding," Marietta said.

I shook my head.

"Wow," Dryser said. "Who'd've thought anything'd be that backward twenty years ago?"

"You had a newspaper then, didn't you?" Bartell asked. "Someone had to notice this."

"We did," I said.

"And there'd be police records or something strange. Big dirt circles don't appear overnight."

"In England they do," Harwell said.

"Those're crop circles," Dryser said. "That's a different phenomenon."

"We don't know that," Marietta said. In her tone, she cited the first rule of investigation. Never assume.

"Listen, Peter," I said. "You're better at research than I am. You go, see what you can find."

"I'll help him," Dryser said. "I'm not going to get much here."

"See if there are aerial photographs of this place," Harwell said.

"Good thought," Dryser said, and then he and Bartell left.

Marietta traced the radiation around the point of the circle. Her readings didn't change. I scanned the area, as I usually did a crash site. Here I found used condoms, a hypodermic, bubblegum wrappers, and a Frisbee. Harwell continued to snap pictures.

I didn't know what I wanted from this work. Richard had known. He had come here, assuming that the circle had been burned into the ground by a flying saucer that came at regular intervals, and took people. He had hoped it might take him, but if his hypothesis were true (and I doubted it was), he would never have been taken. All the disappeared were in states of flux. They had no one place where they belonged. I would have had a better chance of disappearing than Richard ever would.

"We need a shovel," Marietta said to no one in particular.

"We need drier clothes," Harwell muttered.

"We need lunch," I said, and led them back to the SUV.

***

FOR THE NEXT THREE DAYS, we researched and hypothesized and worked. We dug into the circle and found that the dirt and the radiation went down at least six feet, but we also discovered nothing else—no debris, no metal, no garbage. It was as if the dirt circle were completely pristine.

Aerial photographs taken during World War II showed a Seavy Village I didn't recognize, a small place that hadn't even grown near Felton Woods. The clearing wasn't visible at all in those photographs. When we used a magnifying glass, we realized the entire area was covered in trees.

The trees disappeared in 1955, and a perfect circle took their place. The topography maps showed an incline where the area was now flat. We had no aerial photographs for the years in between, so Bartell and Dryser had to search records until they found mention of the dirt circle.

The first mention appeared in the *Oregonian* in December, 1952. Apparently a loud explosion was heard in Felton Woods late the night of December 30, and fire crews were called to put out a raging fire near the creek. Local papers did not report this, nor did the *Oregonian* do any follow-ups. Later newspaper histories of Felton Woods mentioned the explosion, but never tied it to any of the strange events. Apparently no one knew what caused the explosion, nor did anyone try to figure it out.

The team got interested here. To them, this was less about UFOs than experimental aircraft. But Bartell researched missing experimental craft, and didn't find anything that had disappeared over Oregon at that time. He didn't even find anything that had disappeared in the Pacific Northwest.

Marietta believed that something with a nuclear payload crashed in Felton Woods and the Air Force kept it quiet. I didn't, though. A nuclear payload like the ones the U.S. used in the early fifties would have created a serious radiation problem, and more than a small circle of dirt and some trees would have been destroyed.

Late one night after the others had gone to sleep, Harwell knocked on my door. I was still awake, staring into the fire, and wondering if the fall storms would ever ease. I had just gotten off the phone with Stacy—she wanted to help us search the wood, but I had said no. The radiation worried me more than I wanted to admit—and I was thinking of turning on the television to see if I could take my mind off things for a while.

When I got up and opened the door, Harwell pushed inside. He had tied his hair back with a thin strip of leather.

He wasn't wearing a shirt, and his feet were bare. He was frowning.

"Tell me," he said. "When you took those Polaroids, did you see the mist in your frame?"

"How the hell should I know?" I asked. "It was twenty-five years ago."

"Think," he said.

"Why? Do you have anything?"

"Not concrete. But tomorrow is a full moon, did you know that?"

Somehow those two thoughts had to be linked, but I didn't know how. "What are you thinking?"

He sank into the easy chair and stuck his feet toward the fire. "I took fifteen photographs of that rock. I had some geology in school. The thing doesn't look like it came from a stream bed or had water flow over it. In fact, it doesn't look any different from the rock you took a picture of."

"Should it?"

He swept a hand to the window. Rain poured down outside, dotting the pain. "Weather like this, and twenty-five years, not to mention an occasional flood from that creek, yeah. It should look different."

My mouth went dry.

"Now maybe I'm as nuts as—." He stopped himself and his eyes flashed an apology.

"As Richard," I finished for him.

"But that rock has bothered me from the beginning. So I started looking at your pictures. It's the knife that's different, right? Has anyone else ever placed a knife on that spot?"

"How the hell should I know?"

"No, I mean, those UFO freaks and those TV people and the Uri Geller fan club. The ones that contacted you."

"Not to my knowledge," I said, not quite sure what he was getting at. "And I think Richard would have made a note of it in his diaries."

"That's what I thought." He leaned forward. "So here's the thing. We replicate the experiment."

"What?"

"I'm no scientist," he said, "but it seems to me the best way to reproduce the results you got is to replicate the experiment. And we have the opportunity to do that tomorrow night."

"It's supposed to rain tomorrow night. It was clear and dry when Richard and I went down to the creek."

"All the better."

"But there can't be ground fog in these conditions."

"Sure there can."

"It's too cold, and too late in the year."

Harwell shrugged. "Then nothing happens. You can't say we didn't try."

True enough. And at least we would be doing something. Right now it felt as if we were spinning our wheels. It was strange to work backwards, strange to have a hypothesis about what might turn out to be nothing.

But I was afraid to return to the fairy circle in the moonlight. I told myself I didn't want to mess with an old memory, but that wasn't it. The fear I hadn't felt as a young boy I'd been feeling ever since. And it was a fear I didn't really want to confront.

Still the others, when consulted, thought it a good idea. I didn't mention my reservations. It wasn't fair, after all. I had asked them to come against their wills, and they had, for me. I couldn't back out on an experiment just because it made me feel uneasy.

That night, as I finally drifted off to sleep, I found myself wondering what I was afraid of, and being unable to answer the question.

***

THE NEXT DAY, a Saturday, dawned clear and cold. The ocean was an electric blue with yellowish gray white caps on its waves. Debris floated near the shore, the remains of several days of storms. The storm promised for this day was still out in the Pacific, moving slowly and possibly dissipating, according to the news.

I went to Cindy's for lunch. I told my team I wanted to check up on the girls, but I also needed to talk to Stacy.

The house was a mess. Even though it was after noon, Cindy still wore her bathrobe. She hadn't washed her hair in days. No one had done the dishes, either, and April was locked in her room once again.

Instead of talking to Stacy, I made her and Heather start the dishes. Then I made Cindy take a shower, and I knocked on April's door. She didn't answer, so I opened it.

She was unconscious on the bed, and nothing I could do could wake her.

I thought about calling an ambulance, but I didn't. It was quicker in Seavy Village—or it had been when I was a boy—to drive her directly. I picked her up and carried her from the room. She was skeletal, and weighed next to nothing. The arm that dangled was no wider than a ruler, and I could see the outlines of all her bones.

"Tell your mom I'm taking April to the emergency room," I said as I slammed through the kitchen. Stacy ran beside me, asking what was wrong, but I was too angry to reply. They were all so wrapped up in their problems that they hadn't seen the girl starving in their midst.

I had seen, but I had thought it all past when April got angry at me. Instead, I spent my time in Felton Woods, just like her father.

I laid April on the back seat, and was about to get up front when Stacy let herself in. "Stay here," I said.

She shook her head. "She's my sister."

I didn't respond. Instead, I backed the car out, and headed down the road at a fast clip.

I still knew the back streets, and I got to the hospital in record time. They took April away from me, and Stacy and I sat for nearly an hour before Cindy and Heather came in, looking frightened.

"Is she going to be all right?" Cindy asked.

This was Richard's legacy, Richard's family, the very thing I had envied of him. "She's malnourished," I said. "She hasn't had anything to drink, they believe, in two days. She had slipped into a coma. She would have died if I hadn't knocked on that door."

Cindy put a hand to her mouth. "You must think I'm a bad mother," she said.

What was the Biblical phrase? It was as if scales fell from my eyes. "No, Cindy," I snapped. "I know you are."

She gasped, and so did Heather. Stacy grabbed my arm. "Uncle Scott—"

I shook away. If I stayed any longer, I would say more things I would later regret. "They'll stabilized her. I'll be back to visit her later."

And then I left.

***

I WENT BACK to the house, and finished cleaning, furious more at myself than at them. They lived their lives. I was the outsider who could see them clearly, and I had done nothing. Or what I had done, I had done wrong. I picked up the towels Cindy left in the bathroom, stripped the sheets off April's bed, and started a load of laundry. I finished the dishes, scrubbed the floors, put everything away, and still I found things to clean. The house hadn't had a complete going over in months, maybe years. My mother would have been appalled. I know I was.

They still hadn't returned when I finished. I almost went back to the Lodge, but something stopped me. I had come to the house to talk to Stacy, to ask for her help. But she was preoccupied now.

I was on my own.

I swallowed, wondering if I should call off the team, or if it was my own fear that was speaking yet again. I leaned my head against the wall, knew that everything was mixed up in my mind—the fairy circle, Richard's death, his family's disintegration. And mixed with it were my feelings for Richard and his for me, all of them focused on that one night, the night when everything changed.

Without even thinking about it, I turned and walked down the hall to what had become Cindy's bedroom. They had a two-sided bureau, and the left side had been Richard's. It had been as long as the two of them had been together. Cindy hadn't been able to do anything since he died. I knew she hadn't clean out his stuff.

It didn't take me long to find the pocket knife. It was hidden in the bottom drawer, inside an old pair of socks. Richard hadn't changed in all the years of his life. Whenever he wanted to hide something, he put it inside a sock in the bottom drawer. I wondered what else I would find, buried there, if I bothered to look.

I slipped the knife into my pocket, then, almost as an afterthought, I took the old Polaroid camera down from its place of honor on the nearby bookshelf. I glanced at the back, and saw that the camera still had some old film in it. I didn't know if the battery was fresh. I didn't care. Something about what Harwell had said about reproducing the experiment and replicating the results reverberated in my mind.

I called the team from the house, told them everything was still on for the night, and then I returned to the hospital. April hadn't yet awakened, but her prognosis was good. Cindy was talking to a child welfare officer, and Stacy looked terrified. Heather was asleep on the waiting room couch.

I stayed with them until Cindy returned. The welfare officer wanted to talk to me as well. We went to an empty room down the hall. She asked me what I thought would be best for the family.

"If I knew that," I said, "I would have already done it."

And then I left.

***

THE TEAM WAS WAITING for me at the Lodge. Marietta took one look at my face and said, "We don't have to do this if you don't want to."

I shook my head. "We've come this far." Then I reached into my pocket, removed the knife and tossed it at Harwell. "May as well reproduce as much as we can."

He caught the knife, then turned it in his hand. With his thumb and forefinger, he pulled open the blade. "Shiny."

"Yeah," I said. "I don't think it was ever used."

But of course I had no way to know that. I had no way to know anything any more.

Marietta made me go to the cafe and have dinner. Then we waited until 11 p.m., which I figured would be about the time that Richard and I walked down the path.

We all piled into the SUV. and drove to the house. The lights were out, but Cindy's car was in the driveway. I made

Dryser park on the road below the house, and I insisted on complete quiet as we snuck through the yard. I didn't want to scare Cindy, and I didn't want to wake Stacy. I didn't want her to join us. The last thing I needed, after that day's tragedy, was to have something happen to my youngest niece.

The path was narrow as always, and this time, no one had tried to block it with branches and cut grass. The ground was muddy and slick, and I indicated to the group to make sure their hands were on something firm before they took a step. The moonlight was as clear as it had been on that singular night in my memory, but the air was colder. I had forgotten gloves, and by the time I was halfway down the path, my fingers were raw.

The distance to the fairy circle from the house was much shorter than I remembered. We reached the dirt in only a few minutes. Bartell shut off our flashlight, and Harwell took out his camera. The whir/click of his work echoed in the small forest. I had the Polaroid around my neck, but I wasn't ready to use it.

My mouth was dry and my hands were shaking. I took the knife, and slowly walked into the middle of the fairy circle.

I expected to slip on muddy ground as I had been doing since I started down the hill, but within the circle, the dirt was crumbly, as if the weeks of rain hadn't happened. The air felt no different here; it was as cold and damp as it had been on the hillside. I bent over the rock.

It was as I remembered, shiny and solid, its seemingly flat surface not flat up close. Now the swirls on the surface didn't look so much like frosting as they did a deliberate pattern, not discernible to the casual eye.

I set the knife across two grooves as I had done all those years before, and then I walked away, picking up the Polaroid as I went. Harwell continued snapping pictures, and I did as well, focusing on the knife.

Beside me, Marietta gasped. So did Dryser. Harwell continued shooting and so did I. Square packets of film spit out of the ancient camera and Bartell caught them before they fell.

Finally I had used up all my film. Harwell had prepared; he had brought several cameras, all with new rolls. When one finished, he picked up another. I let the Polaroid fall to my chest.

The rock was completely covered in white mist. The mist seemed to be growing, expanding, until it filled the fairy circle. In the center was the boulder, the only solid item that I could see. Within the mist, someone—something—had picked up the knife. It floated, free, like the needle on a compass.

Dryser put his hand on my arm and pulled me away from the circle. Then he did the same for Marietta and Bartell. Harwell wouldn't move. He kept photographing everything.

A wave of cold came off that mist so intense that it felt like we had stepped into a deep freeze. Dryser kept backing us up until we could no longer feel the cold. Harwell was shaking. I went to him, grabbed him, and pulled him back as well.

At that moment, a face formed in the mist. It was obsidian, like the rock, and its eyes were yellow. It watched the both of us, and then it dissolved into particles.

"Son of a bitch," Dryser whispered.

"What?" Harwell asked. He looked out of his view frame and swore softly. "When did that mist show up?"

"The whole time," I said. "It's been there since I put the knife down."

"No," he said.

But it had. I picked up my Polaroid and looked through the viewfinder. Nothing. The night was clear, and the moonlight was falling across the rock. Only the knife remained, floating above it, turning, pointing at us as it did so. When I removed the camera, the mist was back.

"That makes no sense," I said. "The viewfinder should see what my eye does."

"It puts one more barrier between the naked eye and the mist," Dryser said.

"Or maybe it's something else," Marietta said. "None of us are scientists."

"I wish we were," Bartell said.

Harwell cursed again, and then replaced a roll of film in one of his cameras. He kept shooting until all his film was gone.

"What do we do now?" he asked.

"We wait," I said.

"For what?"

I shrugged. I had no idea what was going to happen next.

***

WE GREW COLDER. The light dimmed as the moon set in the west. The mist was fading as well. At just about the moment I was going to give up, the knife tilted, point down, and fell into the rock.

It landed with a thud, and then the rock split open. Light poured out. Real light, not the silvery moon stuff. The obsidian face we had seen earlier appeared again, this time attached to a head, a neck and a torso with two arms. It pulled itself out of the split rock and stared at us, golden eyes blinking.

"What do we do now?" Marietta whispered. "Say we came in peace?"

The creature crawled off the side of the rock and along a diagonal through the air, as if it were walking along the side of a building. When it reached the end of the fairy circle, it jumped to the ground. It sat there, as if it were waiting for something.

"Like a person does when faced with a pack of wild animals," Dryser muttered. He had obviously been thinking the same thing I was.

"A person facing a pack of wild animals hauls out a gun," Bartell whispered.

"Not if he wants to tame them," I said. I crouched and reached out a hand. Marietta slapped it away.

"No," she whispered. "What would your family do if you died here too?"

I wanted to argue, but couldn't. Instead she reached out to the creature. Their fingers met, and then went right through each other as if they were two holograms attempting to touch.

"My god," she said, and brought her hand back.

The creature tilted its head. It seemed sad somehow, as if it wanted more. Then it stood and climbed up the air as if it were climbing on something solid. When it reached the edge of the rock, it dipped its head inside.

"What's it doing?" Dryser asked.

"Preparing to take us away," Marietta said.

"It's never hurt a group before," Bartell said.

"That we know of," I said.

Harwell was digging through his bag for more film. His movements were quick, frantic, as if he were looking for a gun.

The creature reached into the rock and grabbed something. Then it braced itself with its remaining hand, and sat up. Balanced on the other hand was a tray. Carefully, like an obsidian waiter in a futuristic cafe, it slid down the nothingness again, until it reached the edge of the fairy circle. Then it dropped the tray onto the ground.

We dove behind trees like extras in a bad war movie. I hit Marietta along the way, knocked her over, and had to drag her with me. We cowered, but nothing happened.

And when I peered around the tree, the entire fairy circle was dark.

"Found some film!" Harwell said.

"Too late," Bartell said. "It's gone."

Dryser grabbed a flashlight and shone it on the circle. Nothing was there, no mist, no obsidian creature. Even the rock looked normal.

Only the knife was missing.

"What did it throw at us?" Marietta asked.

"Let's go see," I said.

"Wait!" Harwell said. He came out from behind his tree, shooting pictures of the entire area. He crouched over the tray, and let out a soft whistle. "Any of this stuff look familiar?"

We came out of our hiding places. The tray was silver in appearance, highly polished, and on it were dozens of small items, from wedding rings to wallets, from dog collars to i.d. bracelets.

"My god," Bartell said.

"Ten to one the names in those wallets'll correspond with the names of the folks who've disappeared," said Dryser.

"What was that creature doing, bragging?" Harwell asked.

"Shut up and take pictures," Dryser said.

"Right." Harwell bent over the tray as if he were doing a spread for *House and Garden*.

"I don't think it was bragging," Marietta said. "I think it was apologizing."

"Apologizing?" I asked.

"Look," she said, pointing at the nearest wallet. "It's got some sort of water damage."

"That's not water," Dryser said. "That's frost."

"Or ice," Bartell said. "Water usually doesn't leave that white film on leather."

"Ice is water," Marietta said.

"We're speculating again," I said.

"What do you expect us to do?" Dryser said. "Knock on the rock and get facts?"

The cold was gone. The air felt normal. I glanced at him, then, without warning the others, stepped into the fairy circle.

"Scott!" Marietta said.

"Stop!" Bartell said.

I didn't listen to them. I crossed to the rock and knocked on it, just like Dryser suggested. The rock was cool to my touch. After a moment, I knocked again.

I thought I heard a corresponding sound coming from inside, but nothing happened. I knocked until the side of my hand was raw, and the rock never opened, never split again.

"Anyone got a knife?" I asked.

Harwell tossed me his. It was a Swiss Army knife, heavier than Richard's and not as pretty. I laid it across the rock as I had laid the other. Then I stood back.

Nothing happened. We waited nearly an hour and nothing happened.

"Maybe it was the moonlight and the knife," Dryser said.

"Maybe it was the silver and pearl handle," Marietta said.

"Maybe it was the timing," Bartell said.

Whatever it was, we couldn't duplicate it that night. Nor the next night, nor the next.

Then, on the third night, fire erupted in Felton Woods, burning the fairy circle and the surrounding trees. No one was injured, but when the smoke cleared, the rock was gone.

***

OF COURSE, now we live in the realm of wackos. I tried to protect the team. I tried to let them fade into the woodwork, and claim that I was alone in the Felton Woods. But they had had an experience they wanted to discuss, and Harwell wanted to defend his photographs—decisions they would all live to regret.

We've been interviewed from everyone in the paranormal media from Art Bell to *Unsolved Mysteries*. We've signed with a studio that wants to make a film from our experience. We've made money. Marietta laughs at me. She says everything I touch turns to gold.

I wish that were true.

The price for all of this has been subtle. The Air Force no longer trusts our service, believing that we're searching for UFOs in the desert, not experimental aircraft. Bartell was quietly asked to leave Northwestern. Annapolis kept Dryser, partly because he was one of the most popular instructors on campus and partly because military folk are more accustomed to strange and unexplained experiences than they lead us to believe. The experience made Marietta a minor celebrity at NASA, something she never really wanted.

I'm the only one who is unchanged, at least professionally. Personally, I have spent more money than I care to think of, putting together a team of scientists to study the events in the Felton Woods. They're hampered by many things, including the anecdotal nature of much of the experience and the fact that the fairy circle is gone.

The night after the fire, the rains came and for the first time in forty years, the fairy circle turned to mud. In the spring, grass pushed its way to the top, and small seedlings sprouted into tiny trees. The radiation was gone as if it had never been.

The watches, the wallets, the wedding rings did indeed come from the missing people. All of the items were damaged in some way. Most authorities think they were frozen and then thawed out, but no one could prove that. The effect would be the same, they say, if some of these things were under the cold mountain run-off in Felton Creek for years.

Interviewers ask me if I have any theories and I tell them I don't. I'm lying. I have a theory. I just don't want to taint my scientists by saying it aloud.

The only person I've shared this idea with is Marietta. She listens sometimes, usually with a healthy skepticism. But on this one, she agrees with me.

I think the aliens—and I do believe they were aliens—had come to the Felton Woods forty years ago, and set up a blind. Jane Goodall from Mars, I guess. They used that blind to study human beings, and they thought they were perfectly safe. After all, except for moments at touchdown and takeoff, their ship existed in a slightly different dimension. No one could touch it. All it did was give off low levels of radiation, except of course for the door or the rock, as we called it, which had to remain in our dimension. The creatures could disguise themselves as mist, and walk among us, observing, studying, learning.

The problem they hadn't expected was the effect of the cold that emanated from their ship at odd moments. I don't know if that was exhaust, or waste being disposed of, or simply a combination of elements, but sometimes, humans, dogs, wolves, got caught in the cold and died—like my brother did. Exposure. Deep cold. Severe trauma to the skin tissue caused by natural elements. Only it masked time of death, and it would have revealed the position of the blind.

So they took the bodies and disposed of them, somehow, in their machine, maybe or in the creek. And they kept identification. Or perhaps the wallets and rings and collars served as souvenirs. I think they managed to dispose of Richard's tent and his things before someone stumbled on his body, just before dawn, but they hadn't taken him yet. They had screwed up, and that led us to them.

Richard and I had stumbled on an accidental way to open their ship. Only that first night, I had grabbed the knife before the entire procedure occurred. Perhaps I had felt fingers against my own as the knife dropped into my hand, or perhaps it was the first stages of the tissue damage that would have led to my death.

I will never know.

What I do know—what I believe and cannot prove—is that my team and I opened that ship. And when we did, the aliens saw us, knew that we had seen them, and knew their experiment was done. All those years of study ended when the creatures they were studying discovered the blind. The aliens could no longer watch in silence. They would have become the studied or, perhaps worse for them, they would have become part of the experiment.

Marietta disagrees with me on fundamentals. She believes they captured and killed the missing people, experimenting on the captives in a Whitley Strieber sort of way to gain a better understanding of human beings. That's why everyone who disappeared was unattached, or whose disappearance could be explained in other ways.

I think that last was merely a coincidence. She says there are no such thing as coincidences. We argue fruitlessly about this. Lack of proof is a serious problem.

The scientists don't even know where the aliens came from. Lately they've been suggesting that the aliens may live on Earth, only in that different dimension. I hate that explanation, and hope they find another. But I doubt we'll learn anything knew.

Of course, I've told all of this to Stacy, and Heather, and April. They don't care. Their mother has been under a psychiatrist's care now for the better portion of the year. Her mental state had been deteriorating when Richard was alive; his death had sent her over an edge that the doctors aren't sure she'll ever come back from.

I have bought a house in the new development near the golf course, and the girls live with me. Families are nothing like I had imagined they would be. From a distance they look completely different—easier, I think, and more orderly. April takes much of my time. She's anorexic, her response to her parents' obsessions. Heather challenges my authority at all times, and Stacy—well, Stacy has made Felton Woods the center of her life. Part of the reason I hired the scientists was so that I could reassure her that someone was working on her father's discovery, that he had not died in vain.

Although I am not sure of that. I think he and I were watching each other from opposite blinds, seeing only that little patch of woods available to our viewfinders. He believed that my life was better, and he tried to emulate it, in his own way, while, at the same time, believing that I had shut off the most important side of myself, the side that needed love and family and warmth.

From my blind, the view was just as narrow, and just as wrong. Richard's family wasn't perfect, and I really didn't know any of its members until he died. But he hadn't squandered his potential, as I had thought. And he faced each and every day with more courage than I had ever given him credit for.

I wonder sometimes what those aliens observed in that wood. The condoms and beer bottles give me some hint. But they must have seen other things, from frightened little boys approaching the circle on a dare to drug addicts shooting up and then acting crazy. Was the alien view of human existence as narrow and limiting as mine of Richard? Or were they savvy enough to know that all they had seen was one small corner of a very large and very complex world?

I don't know. I will never know, no matter how many scientists I buy, no matter how many hours they work in studying events in the Felton Woods.

For I am glimpsing the aliens from my own little blind, and my observation of them is even shorter than their observation of me and mine. And that is why I do not talk about them, except when I need to help out my friends, to support them as they go from talk show to talk show, from one well-paying but weird project to another.

Some of those shows say the greatest mystery of Felton Woods is what I think about the events. But that's not true. The greatest mystery of Felton Woods is why the aliens chose that spot, and stayed there for so long.

The next great mystery is why no one exposed them before we did.

I find myself thinking that we're like deer going about our business in the forest. We walk the same paths and do not look around us. And when we do look, we don't like what we see.

I know I don't like what I've seen. Not the aliens or Richard's family or the changes in my friends. I'm not referring to that. What I've seen is deeper, and more personal. My experiences in Felton Woods showed me the depth of my own ignorance.

And it astounds me.

Discovery

"OVER THERE." Pita Cardenas waved a hand at the remaining empty spot on the floor of her office. The Federal Express deliveryman rested a hand on top of the stack of boxes on his handcart.

"I don't think it'll fit."

It probably wouldn't. Her office was about the size of the studio apartment she'd had when she went to law school in Albuquerque. She could have had a cubicle with more square footage if she'd taken the job that La Jolla, Webster, and Garcia offered her when she graduated from law school five years before.

But her mother had been dying, and had refused to leave Rio Gordo. So Pita had come back to the town she thought she'd escaped from, put out her shingle, and had gotten a handful of cases, enough to pay the rent on this sorry excuse for an office. If she'd wanted something bigger, she would have had to buy, and even at Rio Gordo's depressed prices, she couldn't afford payments on the most dilapidated building in town.

She stood up. The Fed Ex guy, who drove here every day from Lubbock, was looking at her with pity. He was trim and tanned, with a deep West Texas accent. If she had been less tired and overwhelmed, she would have flirted with him.

"Let's put this batch in the bathroom," she said and led the way through the rabbit path she'd made between the boxes. The Fed Ex guy followed, dragging the six boxes on his hand truck and probably chafing at the extra time she was costing him.

She opened the door. He put the boxes inside, tipped an imaginary hat to her, and left. She'd have to crawl over them to get to the toilet, but she'd manage.

Six boxes today, twenty yesterday, thirty the day before. Dwyer, Ralbotten, Seacur and Czolb was burying her in paper.

Of course, she had expected it. She was a solo practitioner in a town whose population probably didn't equal the number of people who worked at DRS&C.

People had told her she was crazy to take this case. But she was crazy like an impoverished attorney. Every other firm in New Mexico had told her client, Nan Hughes, to settle. The problem was that Nan didn't want to settle. Settling meant losing everything she owned.

Pita took the case and charged Nan two thousand dollars, with more due and owing when (if) the case went to trial. Pita didn't plan on taking the case to trial. At trial, she wouldn't just get creamed, she'd be pureed, sautéed and recycled.

But she did plan to work for that two grand. She would spend exactly one month filing motions, doing depositions, and listening to offers. She figured once she had actual numbers, she'd be able to convince Nan to take a deal.

If not, she'd resign and wish Nan luck finding a new attorney.

Her actions wouldn't hurt Nan. Nan had a spectacular loser of a case. She was taking on the railroads and two major insurance companies. She had no idea how bad things could get.

Pita would show her. Nan wouldn't exactly be happy with her lot—how could she be, when she'd lost her husband, her business, and her home on the same day?—but she would finally understand how impossible the winning was.

Pita was doing her a favor and making a little money besides.

And what was wrong with that?

***

AT ITS HEART, the case was simple. Ty Hughes tried to beat a train and failed. He survived long enough to leave his wife a voice mail message, which Pita had heard in all its heartbreaking slowness:

"Nan baby, I tried to beat it. I thought I could beat it."

Then his diesel truck engine caught fire and he died, horribly alive, in the middle of the wreck.

The accident occurred on a long stretch of brown nothingness on the New Mexico side of the Texas/New Mexico border. A major highway ran a half mile parallel to the tracks. On the opposite side of the tracks stood the Hughes ranch and all its outbuildings.

Nan Hughes and the people who worked her spread watched the accident. She didn't answer her cell because she'd left it on the kitchen counter in her panic to get down the dirt road where her husband's cattle truck had been demolished by a fast-moving train.

And not just any train.

This train pulled dozens of oil tankers.

It was a miracle the truck engine fire hadn't spread to the tankers and the entire region hadn't exploded into one great fireball.

Pita had been familiar with the case long before Nan Hughes came to her. For weeks, the news carried stories about dead cattle along the highway, the devastated widow, the ruined ranch, and the angry railroad officials who had choice (and often bleeped) words about the idiots who tried to race trains.

It didn't matter that the crossing was unmarked. Even if Ty hadn't left that confession on Nan's voice mail (which she had deleted but which the cell company was so thoughtfully able to retrieve), trains in this part of the country were visible for miles in either direction.

The railroads wanted the ranch, the cattle (what was left of them), the life insurance money, and millions from the ranch's liability insurance. The liability insurance company was willing to settle for a simple million, and the other law firms had told Nan to sell the ranch, and pay the railroads from the proceeds. That way she could live on Ty's life insurance and move away from the site of the disaster.

But Nan kept saying that Ty would haunt her if she gave in. That he had never raced a train in his life. That he knew how far away a train was by its appearance against the horizon—and that he had taught her the same trick.

When Pita gently asked why Ty had confessed to trying to beat the train, Nan had burst into tears.

"Something went wrong," she said. "Maybe he got stuck. Maybe he hadn't looked up. He was in shock. He was dying. He was just trying to talk to me one last time."

Pita could hear any good lawyer tear that argument to shreds, just using Ty's wording. If Ty wanted to talk with her, why hadn't he told her he loved her? Why had he talked about the train?

Pita had gently asked that too. Nan had looked at her from across the desk, her wet cheeks chapped from all the tears she'd shed.

"He knew I saw what happened. He wanted me to know he never would have done that to me on purpose."

In this context, "on purpose" had a lot of different definitions. Ty Hughes probably didn't want his wife to see him die in a train wreck, certainly not in a train wreck he caused. But he had crossed a railroad track with a double-decker cattle truck filled carrying two hundred head. He had no acceleration, and no maneuverability.

He'd taken a gamble, and he'd lost.

At least, Nan hadn't seen the fire in the cab. The truck had flipped over the train, landing on the highway side of the tracks, and had been impossible to see from the ranch side. Whatever Ty Hughes's last few minutes had looked like, Nan had missed them.

She had only her imagination, her anger at the railroads, and her unshakeable faith in her dead husband.

Those were not enough to win a case of this magnitude.

If someone asked Pita what her case really was (and if this imaginary someone could get her to answer honestly), what she'd say was that she was going to try Ty Hughes before his wife, and show her how impossible a defense of the man's actions that morning would be in court.

And Pita believed her own powers of persuasion were enough to convince her jury of one to settle.

***

BUT THE BOXES were daunting. In them were bits and pieces of information, reproduced letters and memos that probably showed some kind of railroad duplicity, however minor. A blot on an engineer's record, for example, or an accident at that same crossing twenty years before.

If Pita had the support of a giant law firm like La Jolla, Webster, and Garcia, she might actually delve into that material. Instead, she let it stack up like unread novels in the home of an obsessive compulsive.

The only thing she did do was take out the witness list, which had come in its own envelope as part of court-ordered discovery. The list had the witnesses' names along with their addresses, phone numbers, and the dates of their depositions. DRS&C was so thorough that each witness had a single line notation at the bottom of the cover sheet describing the reason the witness had been deposed in this case.

The list would help Pita in her quest to recreate the accident itself. She had dozens of questions. Had someone inspected the truck to see if it malfunctioned at the time of the accident? Why had Ty stayed in the truck when it was clear that it was going to catch fire? How badly had he been injured? How good was Ty's eyesight? And how come no one helped him before the truck caught fire?

She was going to cover all her bases. All she needed was one argument strong enough to let Nan keep the house.

She was afraid she might not even find that.

DRS&C's categories were pretty straightforward. They had categories for the ranch, the railroad, and the eyewitnesses.

A number of the witnesses belonged to separate lawsuits, started because of the fender benders on the nearby highway. About a dozen cars had damage—some while they were stopped beside the road, and others because they'd been going too fast to stop when the train accident occurred.

Pita started charting the location of the cars as she figured this category out, and realized all of them had been in the far inside lane, going east. People who had pulled over to help Ty and the railroad employees had instead been dealing with accidents involving their own cars.

A separate group of accident victims had resolved insurance claims: their vehicles had been hit or had hit a cow that had escaped from the cattle truck. One poor man had had his SUV gored by an enraged bull.

Cars heading west had had an easier time of things. None had hit each other and a few had stopped. Of those who had stopped, some were listed as 911 callers. One had grabbed a fire extinguisher and eventually tried to put out the truck cab fire. That person had prevented the fire from spreading to the tankers.

But the category that caught Pita's attention was a simple one. Several people on the list had been marked "Witness," with no accompanying explanation.

One had an extra long zip code, and as she entered it into her own computer data base, she realized that the last three digits weren't part of the zip code at all.

They were a previous notation, one that hadn't been deleted.

Originally, this witness had been in the 911 category.

She decided to start with him.

***

C.P. WILLIAMS was a Texas financier of the Houston variety, even though his offices were in Lubbock. He wore cowboy boots, but they were custom made, hand-tooled jobbies that wouldn't last fifteen minutes on a real ranch. He had an oversized silver belt buckle and he wore a bolo tie, but his shiny suit was definitely not off the rack and neither was the silk shirt underneath it. His cufflinks matched his belt buckle and he twisted them as he led Pita into his office.

"I already gave a deposition," he said.

"Before I was on the case," Pita said.

His office was big, with original oil paintings of the Texas Hill Country, and a large but not particularly pretty view of downtown Lubbock.

"Can't you just read it?" He slipped behind a custom-made desk. The chair in front was made of hand-tooled leather that made her think of his impractical boots.

She sat down. The leather pattern bit through the thin pants of her best suit.

"I have a few questions of my own." She took out a small tape recorder. "I may have to call you in for a second deposition, but I hope not."

Mostly because she would have to rent space as well as a court reporter in order to conduct that deposition. Right now, she simply wanted to see if any testimony was worth the extra cost.

"I don't have that much time. I barely have enough time to see you now." He glanced at his watch for emphasis.

She clicked on the recorder. "Then let's do this quickly. Please state your name and occupation for the record."

He did.

When he finished, she said, "On the morning of the accident—"

"I never saw that damn accident," he said. "I told the other lawyers that."

She was surprised. Why had they talked with him then? She was interviewing blind. So she went with the one fact she knew.

"You called 911. Why?"

"Because of the train," he said.

"What about the train?"

"Damn thing was going twice as fast as it should have been."

For the first time since she'd taken this case, she finally felt a flicker of real interest. "Trains speed?"

"Of course trains speed," he said. "But this one wasn't just speeding. It was going well over a hundred miles an hour."

"You know that because…?"

"I was going 70. It passed me. I had nothing else to do, so I figured out the rate of passage. Speed limits for trains on that section of track is 65. Most weeks, the trains match me, or drop back just a bit. This one was leaving me in the dust."

She was leaning forward. If the train was speeding—and if she could prove it—then the accident wasn't Ty's fault alone. He wouldn't have been able to judge how fast the train was going. And if it was going twice as fast as usual, it would have reached him two times quicker than he expected.

"So why call 911?" she asked. "What can they do?"

"Not damn thing," he said. "I just wanted it on record when the train derailed or blew through a crossing or hit some kid on the way to school."

"You could have contacted the railroad or maybe the NTSB," she said. "They could have fined the operators or pulled the engineers off the train."

"I could have," he said. "I didn't want to."

She frowned. "Why not?"

"Because I wanted the record."

And because he repeated that sentence, she felt a slight shiver. "Have you done this before? Clocked trains going too fast, I mean."

"Yeah." He sounded surprised at the question. "So?"

"Do you call 911 on people speeding in cars?"

His eyes narrowed. "No."

"So why do you call on trains?"

"I told you. The potential damage—"

"Did you contact the police after the accident, then?" she asked.

"No. It was already on record. They could find it. That attorney did."

"I wouldn't know how to compute how fast a train was going while I was driving," she said. "I mean, if we were going the same speed or something close, sure. But not an extra thirty miles an hour or more. That's quite a trick."

"Simple math," he said. "You had to do problems like that in school. We all did."

"I suppose," she said. "But it's not something I would think to do. Why did you?"

For the first time, he looked down. He didn't say anything.

"Do you have something against the railroad?" she asked.

His head shot up. "Now you sound like them."

"Them?"

"Those other lawyers."

She started to nod, but made herself stop. "What did they say?"

His lips thinned. "They said that I'm just making stuff up to get the railroad in trouble. They said that I'm pathetic. Me! I out earn half those walking suits. I make money every damn day, and I do it without investing in any land holdings or railroad companies. They have no idea who I am."

Neither did she, really, but she thought she'd humor him.

"You're a good citizen," she said.

"Damn straight."

"Trying to protect other citizens."

"That's right."

"From the railroads."

"They think they can run all over the countryside like they're invulnerable. That train pulling oil tankers, imagine if it had derailed in that accident. You'd've heard the explosion in Rio Gordo."

Probably seen it too. He had a point.

"Tell me," she said. "Is there any way we can prove the train was going that fast?"

"The 911 call," he said.

"Besides the 911 call," she said.

He leaned back as he considered her question. "I'm sure a lot of people saw it. Or you could examine that truck. You know, it's just basic physics. If you vary the speed of an incoming train in an impact with a similar truck frame, you'll get differing results. I'm sure you can find some experts to testify."

You could find experts to testify on anything. But she didn't say that. She was curious about his expertise, though. He seemed to know a lot about trains.

She asked, "Wouldn't a train derail at that speed when it hit a truck like that?"

"Actually, no. It would be less likely to derail when it was going too fast. That truck was a cattle truck, right? If the train hit the cattle car and not the cab, then the train would've treated that truck like tissue. Most cattle cars are made of aluminum. At over a hundred miles per hour, the train would have gone through it like paper."

Interesting. She would check that.

"One last question, Mr. Williams. When did the railroad fire you?"

He blinked at her, stunned. She had caught him. That's why DRS&C's attorneys had called him pathetic. Because he had a reason for his train obsession.

A bad reason.

"That was a long time ago," he whispered.

But she still might be able to use him if he had some kind of expertise. If his old job really did require that he clock trains by sight alone.

"What did you do for them?"

He coughed, then had the grace to finally meet her gaze. "I was a security guard at the station here in Lubbock."

Security guard. Not an engineer, not anyone with special training. Just a guy with a phony badge and a gun.

"That's when you learned to clock trains," she said.

He smiled. "You have to do something to pass the time."

She bit back her frustration. For a few minutes, he'd given her some hope. But all she had was a fired security guard with a grudge.

She wrapped up the interview as politely as she could, and headed into the bright Texas sunshine.

And allowed herself one small moment to wish that C.P. Williams had been a real witness, one that could have opened this case wide.

Then she sighed, and went back to preparing her case for her jury of one.

***

MOST EVERYONE ELSE in the witness category on DRS&C's list was either a rubbernecker or someone who had made a false 911 call. Pita had had no idea how many people reported a crime or an accident *after* seeing coverage of it on television, but she was starting to learn.

She was also learning why the police didn't fine or arrest these people. Most of them were certifiably crazy.

Pita was beginning to think the list was worthless. Then she interviewed Earl Jessup Jr.

Jessup was a contractor who had been on his way to Lubbock to pick up a friend from the airport when he'd seen the accident. He'd pulled over, and because he was so well known in Rio Gordo, someone had remembered he was there.

When Pita arrived at his immaculate house in one of Rio Gordo's failed housing developments, she promised herself she wouldn't interview any more witnesses. Then Jessup pulled the door open. He smiled in recognition. So did she.

She had talked with him in the hospital cafeteria during her mother's final surgery. He'd been there for his brother, who'd been in a particularly horrendous accident, and who had somehow managed to survive.

They hadn't exchanged names.

He was a small man with brown hair in need of a good trim. His house smelled faintly of cigarette smoke and aftershave. The living room had been modified—lowered furniture, and wide paths cut through what had once been wall-to-wall carpet.

"Your brother moved in with you, huh?" she asked.

"He needed somebody," Jessup said with a finality that closed the subject.

He led her into the kitchen. On the right side of the room, the cabinets had been pulled from the walls. A dishwasher peeked out of the debris. On the left were frames for lowered countertops. Only the sink, the stove and the refrigerator remained intact, like survivors in a war zone.

He pulled a chair out for her at the kitchen table. The table was shorter than regulation height. An ashtray sat near the end of the table, but no chair. That had to be where his brother usually parked.

Pita pulled out her tape recorder and a notebook. She explained again why she was there, and asked Jessup to state some information for the record. She implied, as she had with all the others, that this informal conversation was as good as being under oath.

Jessup smiled as she went through her spiel. He seemed to know that his words would have no real bearing on the case unless he was giving a formal deposition.

"I didn't see the accident," he said. "I got there after."

He'd missed the fender benders and the first wave of the injured cows. He'd pulled up just as the train stopped. He'd been the one to organize the scene. He'd sent two men east and two men west to slow traffic until the sheriff arrived.

He'd made sure people in the various accidents exchanged insurance information, and he got the folks who'd suffered minor bumps and bruises to the side of the road. He directed a couple of teenagers to keep an eye on the injured animals, and make sure none of them made for the road again.

Then he'd headed down the embankment toward the overturned truck.

"It wasn't on fire yet?"

"No," he said. "I have no idea how it got on fire."

She frowned. "It overturned. It was leaking diesel and the engine was on."

"So the fancy Dallas lawyers tell me," he said.

"You don't believe them?"

"First thing any good driver does after an accident is shut off his engine."

"Maybe," she said. "If he's not in shock. Or seriously injured. Or both."

"Ty had enough presence of mind to make that phone call." Everyone in Rio Gordo knew about that call. Some even cursed it, thinking Nan could own the railroads if Ty hadn't picked up his cell. "He would've shut off his engine."

Pita wasn't so sure.

"Besides, he wasn't in the cab."

That caught her attention. "How do you know?"

"I saw him. He was sitting on some debris halfway up the road. That's why I was in no great hurry to get down there. He'd gotten himself out, and there wasn't much I could do until the ambulance arrived."

Jessup had a construction worker's knowledge of injuries. He knew how to treat bruises and he knew what to do for trauma. He'd talked with her about that in the cafeteria, when he'd told her how helpless he'd felt coming on his brother's car wrapped around a utility pole. He hadn't been able to get his brother out of the car—the ambulance crew later used the jaws of life—and he was afraid his brother would bleed out right there.

"But you went to help Ty anyway," Pita said.

Jessup got up, walked to the stove, and lifted up the coffee pot. He'd been brewing the old-fashioned way, in a percolator, probably because he didn't have any counter space.

"Want some?" he asked.

"Please," she said, thinking it might get him to talk.

He pulled two mugs out of the dishwasher, then set them on top of the stove. "I thought he was going to be fine."

"You're not a doctor. You don't know." She wasn't acting like a lawyer now. She was acting like a friend, and she knew it.

He grabbed the pot, and poured coffee into both mugs. Then he brought them to the table.

"I did know," he said. "I knew there was trouble, and I left."

"Sounds like you did a lot before you left," she said, trying to move him past this. She remembered long talks about his guilt over his brother's accident. "Organizing the people, making sure Ty was okay. Seems to me that you did more than most."

He shook his head.

"What else could you have done?" she asked.

"I could've gone down there and helped him," he said. "If nothing else, I could've defended him against those men with guns."

She went cold. Men with guns. She hadn't heard about men with guns.

"Who had guns?" she asked.

He gave her a self-deprecating smile, apparently realizing how dramatic he had sounded. "Everyone has guns. This is the Texas-New Mexico border."

He'd said too much, and he clearly wanted to backtrack. She wouldn't let him.

"Not everyone uses them at the scene of an accident," she said.

"If they'd've been smart, they might have. That bull was mighty scary."

"Who had guns?" she asked.

He sighed, clearly knowing she wouldn't back down. "The engineers. They carried their rifles out of the train."

She raised her eyebrows, not sure what to say.

He seemed to think she didn't believe him, so he went on. "I figured they were carrying the guns to shoot any livestock that got in their way. Made me want my gun. I'd been thinking about the accident, not a bunch of injured animals that weighed eight times what I did."

"Why did you leave?" she asked.

"It was a judgment call," he said. "I was watching those engineers walk. With purpose."

As she listened to Jessup recount the story, she realized the purpose had nothing to do with cattle. These men carried their rifles like they intended to use them. They weren't looking at the carnage. After they'd finished inspecting the train for damage, they didn't look at the train either.

Instead, they stared at Ty.

"For the entire two-mile walk?" she asked.

"I don't know," Jessup said. "That's when I decided not to stay. I thought Ty was going to be fine."

He paused. She waited, knowing if she pushed him, he might not say any more.

Jessup ran a hand through his hair. "I knew that in situations like this tempers get out of hand. I couldn't be the voice of reason. I might even get some of the blame."

He wrapped his hands around his coffee mug. He hadn't touched the liquid.

"Besides," he said, "I could see Ty's cowboys. They were riding around the train and heading toward the loose cattle near the highway. If things got ugly, they could help him. I headed back up the embankment, went to my truck, and drove on to Lubbock."

"Then I don't understand why this is bothering you," she said. "You did as much as you could, and then you left it to others, the ones who needed to handle the problem."

"Yeah," he said softly. "I tell myself that."

"But?"

He tilted his head, as if shaking some thoughts loose. "But a couple of things don't make sense. Like why did Ty go back into the cab of that truck? And how come no one smelled the diesel? Wouldn't it bother them so close to the oil tankers?"

She waited, watching him. He shrugged.

"And then there's the nightmares."

"Nightmares?" she asked.

"I get into my truck, and as I slam the door, I hear a gunshot. It's half a second behind the sound of the door slamming, but it's clear."

"Did you really hear that?" she asked.

"I like to think if I did, I would've gone back. But I didn't. I just drove away, like nothing had happened. And a friend of mine died."

He didn't say anything else. She took another sip of her coffee, careful not to set the mug to close to her recorder.

"No one else reported gunshots," she said.

He nodded.

"No one else saw Ty outside that cab," she said.

"He was in a gully. I was the only one who went down the embankment. You couldn't see him from the road."

"And the truck? Could you see it?"

He shook his head.

"What do you think happened?" she asked.

"I don't know," he said, "and it's driving me insane."

***

IT BOTHERED HER TOO, but not in quite the same way.

She found Jessup in DRS&C's list of 911 nutcases. He'd been buried among the crazies, just like important information was probably hidden in the boxes that littered her office floor.

No one else had seen the angry engineers or Ty out of the truck, but no one could quite figure out how he'd made that cell phone call either. If he'd been sitting on some debris outside the cab, that made more sense than calling from inside, while bleeding, with the engine running and diesel dripping.

But Jessup was right. It raised some disturbing questions.

They bothered her, enough so that she called Nan on her cell phone during the drive back to her office.

"Do you have a copy of the autopsy report for Ty?" Pita asked.

"There was no autopsy," Nan said. "It's pretty clear how he died."

Pita sighed. "What about the truck? What happened to it?"

"Last I saw, it was in Digger's Salvage Yard."

So Pita pulled into the salvage yard, and parked near a dented Toyota. Digger was a good ole boy who salvaged parts, and when he couldn't, he used a crusher to demolish the vehicles into metal for scrap.

But he still had the cab of that truck—insurance wouldn't release it until the case was settled.

For the first time, she looked at the cab herself, but couldn't see anything except charred metal, a steel frame, and a ruined interior. She wasn't an expert, and she needed one.

It took only a moment to call an old friend in Albuquerque who knew a good freelance forensic examiner. The examiner wanted $500 plus expenses to travel to Rio Gordo and look at the truck.

Pita hesitated. She could've – and should've – called Nan for the expense money.

But the examiner's presence would raise Nan's hopes. And right now, Pita couldn't do that. She was trusting a man she'd met late night at the hospital, a man who talked her through her mother's last illness, a man she couldn't quite get enough distance from to examine his veracity.

She needed more than Jessup's nightmares and speculations. She needed something that might pass for proof.

***

"I can't tell you when it got there," said the examiner, Walter Shepard. He was a slender man with intense eyes. He wore a plaid shirt despite the heat and tan trousers that had pilled from too many washings.

He was sitting in Pita's office. She had moved some boxes aside so that the path into the office was wider. She'd also found a chair that had been buried since the case began.

He pushed some photographs onto her desk. The photographs were close-ups of the truck's cab. He'd thoughtfully drawn an arrow next to the tiny hole in the door on the driver's side.

"It's definitely a bullet hole. It's too smooth to be anything else," he said. "And there's another in the seat. I was able to recover part of a bullet."

He shifted the photos so that she could see a shattered metal fragment.

"The problem is I can't tell you anything else, except that the bullet holes predate the fire. I can't tell you how long they were there or how they got there. They could be real old. Or brand new. I can't tell."

"That's all right." A bullet hole, along with Jessup's testimony, was enough to cast doubt on everything. She felt like she could go to DRS&C and ask for a settlement.

She wasn't even regretting that she hadn't worked on contingency. This case was proving easier than she had thought it would be.

"I know you asked me to look for evidence of shooting or a fight," Shepard said, "but I wouldn't be doing my job if I let it go at that. The anomaly here isn't the bullets. It's the fire itself."

She looked up from the photos, surprised. Shepard wasn't watching her. He was still studying the photographs. He put a finger on one of them.

"The diesel leaked. There's runoff along the tank and a drip pattern that trails to the passenger side of the cab."

The cab had landed on its passenger side.

"But the fire started here." He was touching the photo of the interior of the cab. He pushed his finger against the image of the ruined seat. "See how the flames spread upwards. You can see the burn pattern. And fuel fed it. It burned around something—probably the body—so it looks to me like someone poured fuel onto the body itself and lit it on fire. I didn't find a match, but I found the remains of a Bic lighter on the floor of the cab. It melted but it's not burned the way everything else is. I think it was tossed in after the fire started."

Pita was having trouble wrapping her mind around what he was saying. "You're saying someone deliberately started the fire? So close to oil tankers?"

"I think that someone knew the truck wouldn't explode. The fire was pretty contained."

"Some people from the highway had a fire extinguisher in their car. It was too late to save Ty."

"You'll want your examiner to look at the body again," Shepard said. "I have a hunch you'll find that your client's husband was dead before he burned, not after."

"Based on this pattern."

"A man doesn't sit calmly and let himself burn to death," Shepard said. "He was able to make a phone call. He was conscious. He would have tried to get out of that cab. He didn't."

Pita was shaking. If this was true, then this case went way beyond a simple accident. If this was true, then those engineers shot Ty and tried to cover it up.

Ballsy, considering how close to the road they had been.

But the other drivers had been preoccupied with their own accidents and the injured cows and stopping traffic.

No one except Jessup had even tried to come down the embankment.

And the engineers, who drove the route a lot, would have known how hard that truck was to see from the road.

They would have figured that the burning cab would get put out once someone saw the smoke. No wonder they'd lit the body. They didn't want to risk catching the cab on fire, and leaving the bullet-ridden corpse untouched.

"You're sure?" Pita asked.

"Positive." Shepard gathered the photos. "If I were you, I'd take this to the state police. You don't have an accident here. You have cold-blooded murder."

***

THE NEXT FEW WEEKS became a blur. DRS&C dropped the suit, becoming the friendliest big law firm that Pita had ever known. Which made her wonder when they'd realized that the engineers had committed murder.

Either way, it didn't matter. DRS&C was willing to work with her, to do whatever it took to "make Mrs. Hughes happy."

Nan wouldn't be happy until her husband's killers were brought to justice. She snapped into action the moment the state coroner confirmed Shepard's hunches. Ty had been shot in the skull before he died, and then his body had been burned to cover up the crime.

If Nan hadn't worked so hard and believed in her husband so much, no one would have known.

The story came out slowly. The train had been speeding when Ty crossed the tracks. Williams' estimate of more than 100 miles per hour was probably correct—enough for the railroads to have liability right there.

But the engineers, both frightened by the accident itself and terrified for their jobs, had walked the length of the train to Ty's overturned truck and, finding him alive and relatively unhurt, let their anger explode.

They'd threatened him with the loss of everything if he didn't confess that he had failed to beat the train. He'd made the call to satisfy them. But it hadn't worked. Somehow—and neither man was going to admit how (not even more than a year later at sentencing)—one of the rifles had gone off, killing him. Then they'd stuffed him in the cab—whose ignition was off—poured some diesel from the spill on him, and lit him on fire.

They watched him burn for a few minutes before going up the embankment to see if anyone had a fire extinguisher in his car. Fortunately someone did. Otherwise, they planned to have someone drive them the two miles to the engine for the train's fire extinguishers.

The engineers were eventually convicted, Nan got to keep her ranch and her husband's reputation, and the railroads kept trying to settle.

But Pita insisted that Nan hire an attorney who specialized in cases against big companies. Pita helped with the hire, finding someone with a great reputation who wasn't afraid of a thousand boxes of evidence and, more importantly, would work on contingency.

"You sure you don't want it?" Nan had asked, maybe two dozen times.

And each time, Pita had said, "Positive. The case is too big for me."

Although it wasn't. She could have gone to La Jolla, Webster, and Garcia as a rainmaker, someone who brought in a huge case and made millions for the company.

But she didn't.

Because this case had taught her a few things.

She'd learned that she hated big cases with lots and lots of evidence.

She'd learned that she really didn't care about the money. (Although the ten thousand dollar bonus that Nan had paid her—a bonus Pita hadn't asked for—had come in very handy.)

And she learned how valuable it was to know the people of her town. If she hadn't spent all those evenings in the cafeteria with Jessup, she wouldn't have trusted his story, and she never would have hired the forensic examiner.

Her mom had been right, all those years ago. Rio Gordo wasn't a bad place. Yeah, it was impoverished. Yeah, it was filled with dust, and didn't have a good nightlife or a great university.

But it did have some pretty spectacular people.

People who congratulated Pita for the next year on her success in the Hughes case. People who now came to her to do their wills or their prenups. People who asked her advice on the smallest legal matters, and believed her when she gave them an unvarnished opinion.

Her biggest case had helped her discover her calling: She was a small town attorney—someone who cared more about the people around her than the money their cases could bring in.

She wouldn't be rich.

But she would be happy.

And that was more than enough.

Stomping Mad
A Spade Conundrum

S HE CALLED HERSELF the Martha Stewart of Science Fiction, and she looked the part: Homecoming-queen pretty with a touch of maliciousness behind the eyes, a fakely tolerant acceptance of everyone fannish, and an ability to throw the best room party at any given Worldcon in any given year.

So when a body was found in her party suite, the case came to me. Folks in fandom call me the Sam Spade of Science Fiction, but I'm actually more like the Nero Wolfe: a man who prefers good food and good conversation, a man who is huge, both in his appetite and in his education. I don't go out much, except to science fiction conventions (a world in and of themselves) and to dinner with the rare comrade. I surround myself with books, computers, and televisions. I do not have orchids or an Archie Goodwin, but I do possess a sharp eye for detail and a critical understanding of the dark side of human nature.

I have, in the past, solved over a dozen cases, ranging from finding the source of a doomsday virus that threatened to shut down the world's largest fan database to discovering who had stolen the Best Artist Hugo two hours before the award ceremony. My reputation had grown during the last British Fantasy Convention when I—an American—worked with Scotland Yard to recover a diamond worth £1,000,000 that a Big Name Fan had forgotten to put in the hotel's safe.

But I had never faced a more convoluted criminal mind until that Friday afternoon at the First Annual Jurassic Parkathon, a media convention held in Anaheim.

***

THE CONVENTION was officially called Dinocon I because Crichton's people, or Spielberg's people, or some studio's people wouldn't give permission to use the Jurassic Park name with a non-sanctioned project. I normally don't get involved with a media con, especially one held in Anaheim, but this one had a million dollar budget and a state-of-the-art computer system, and I simply couldn't resist the challenge.

So I was in Ops with most of the folks running the con when the call came through. Ops, for those of you who've never seen one, is a hotel function room with most of the furniture removed, replaced with tables covered with computer equipment, too many chairs, and tons of print out paper. Most of the people working Ops look haggard and stressed by the time the convention starts, and many of them are ready to collapse by the time it's over. So we really didn't need to hear some security person, young by the sound of him, on the two-way radio:

"Hey, ah, we got a, um, Situation X, here."

Everyone in Ops snapped to attention. The actual term was a File X—always a pun, everything a pun—and it was only supposed to be used for an extreme emergency.

"Copy that," Doris, a muscular woman the size of Stallone, said. She headed security, and had at every major con I'd ever worked on. Security is important at sf conventions, perhaps *the* most important thing, because these cons, as most of you know, aren't your simple suit-tie-and-briefcase affairs. The big conventions have three levels: the fans, most of whom dress in costume (some medieval barbarians, some Captain Kirk, some space aliens); the pros, most of whom write, act, or somehow work in the science fiction field; the dealers, most of whom sell sf paraphernalia—books, videos, posters, and the ubiquitous Bajoran earrings. Media cons had more earrings, videos, and actors; fewer books, writers, and intellectual discussions. Behind it all is the con-com, the army of people who run the entire shebang, and put out any and all fires along the way. Security deals with most of those: from regular hotel guests who are scared by the werewolf in the elevator to the teenagers who've stayed up all night playing the card game *Magic*, and who suddenly think it fun to pull the fire alarm on the second floor.

Never, in my twenty years of fandom, have we gotten a call for this kind emergency, and never have I heard a security person sound so scared.

"It's in room 4708. Can someone come here?" The security kid's voice cracked, confirming my suspicion: he was a volunteer, and he was eighteen at most.

"What's the nature of the emergency?" Doris asked.

"I don't think you want me to describe it on an open channel," the kid said.

"All right, be right there," Doris said, and left.

We mused about the "Situation" X for a moment. "Maybe," Ruth, the con chair, said, "he saw a fur bikini for the first time."

"It's the masquerade tonight," John said behind her, and we all laughed. He probably saw a costume, got scared, and decided to call it in. We'd all had that happen before.

"Or maybe it's pea soup," said Ben, and I, being most senior on the staff, groaned. I remembered that one, which had now eased into fannish legend. Just after *The Exorcist* came out, some fans in Baltimore held a room party and served pea soup along with the usual potato chips, cheese, and beer. After midnight, when the crowd got really drunk, someone had the brilliant idea of imitating Linda Blair in the famous vomit sequence. Of course, everyone had to do it, and by the time security arrived, a sea of pea soup was running down the corridor like the Blob without the assistance of the special effects people.

"Please, ghod, anything but that," I said.

At that moment, the phone rang. Ruth answered, and handed it to me, her tired face filled with confusion and surprise. "It's Doris," she said. "For you."

I slid my chair back and grabbed the phone, feeling as confused as Ruth looked. Doris could have radioed me. That would have been procedure. Maybe something was really up in 4708.

"Yeah?" I said.

"Spade," she said—my fannish friends had called me Spade since I solved the first case almost twelve years before—"you've gotta come up here. Now."

"What's going on?" I asked.

"An absolute disaster," she said, and hung up.

"Why didn't she use the radio?" Ruth asked.

I shrugged. "I guess she didn't want anyone else wandering up to the room." I eased myself out of my special chair, the one that I insist a con-com bring to every convention if they want my services, and with a push of a button, shut down the financial files on Dinocon's main computer. Then I made my way slowly—because I never hurry—to the fourth floor of the main convention hotel.

Dinocon had 8,000 registered attendees, and it was only Friday afternoon. The convention was scheduled to go through Sunday, and another 2,000 people were expected at the door on Saturday. Most of these folks were already crowding the halls, having conversations with friends they hadn't seen for a while and trying to discover where that night's parties would be held. I squeezed my way through—negotiating packed hallways was never easy for a man of my bulk—and made it to the elevator in time to nab the last spot. No one complained, though, as I squooshed people toward the back. Part of that was my con-com badge—regular con attendees knew better than to harass a person in a con-com badge—and part of it was my reputation.

"Hey, Spade!" someone yelled from the back. "You get a piece of that diamond?"

"I don't charge for my services," I said, in a gently chiding voice. I made my money years ago as an early employee of Microsoft. I took all my bonuses in stock, and then retired at the age of 31, not as rich as Bill Gates, but rich enough.

"He's a gentleman detective," someone else said from the back, and the entire elevator chuckled.

"Imagine," I said as the doors opened on four, "a gentleman—and a scholar."

I got off, but not before I heard more giggling as the doors closed. Fannish humor was not the stuff of stand-up routines, but it was usually full of sweet, if not always socially adept, affection.

The room 4708 was on what had been designated by the hotel as a party floor. On these floors, it was okay to have loud conversation all night, to serve beer in rooms, and to talk in the hallways. Other floors, the non-party floors, were for people who actually wanted to sleep during the con, something I hadn't done in the last thirteen conventions I had attended.

Photocopied 8"x11" signs were taped onto the wallpaper, most of them announcing bid parties for other conventions. The signs on 4708 looked professionally done on slick glossy paper. They announced the first annual

Literature Con to be held in an ancient Hilton an hour outside of Manhattan. I stared at the signs for a moment, frowning. Anyone with half a brain knew that most of Dinocon's attendees weren't likely to attend a literature con, especially one held all the way across the country. But the posters had another draw besides their slick appearance.

Food.

Come to our bid party, the sign read, *and dine at your heart's content. Award-winning chocolates, Lucinda's World Famous Chili, and gourmet dishes from the farthest reaches of the Solar System. Come to* the *party of the convention. You'll talk about it for the next three lifetimes.*

Curiouser and curiouser. Lucinda was Lucinda Danielle Stanhope, also known as the Martha Stewart of Science Fiction. Lucinda hated media cons, thinking that they ruined "pure" science fiction. Pure science fiction, to her, was anything beautifully written with long treatises on science. She thought plot-driven fiction an abomination, and sf on movies and television beneath her notice.

Although she might have changed that opinion, since her current boyfriend, who had started as Science Fiction's answer to James Joyce, had gotten a job as a story consultant for a major studio. ("A guy has to make a buck," he said to me at the last Worldcon. "Besides, since *Independence Day*, everyone is hot for sf properties.")

She might have changed her opinion, but I doubted it.

I had known Lucinda for a long time. She and I had had a run-in at Con Diego (called Con Digeo by its attendees because of all the typos in the program book) several years back and I had tried, unsuccessfully, to avoid her ever since. Our conversations from that day on had consisted of only two words, uttered in passing.

Asshole, she say.

Bitch, I'd respond.

I sighed, squared my shoulders, and braced myself for the verbal onslaught as I knocked on the door.

Doris answered. She looked grim and shaky. She motioned me inside and closed the door.

The suite smelled of fresh bread, chili, and something foul, something I had never smelled before and wasn't sure I wanted to smell again. We stood in an entry that led to the bathroom on the left, a main room just before me, and a bedroom on the right. The security kid so skinny he was skeletal and a shade of green I'd never seen outside of a blacklight poster, leaned against a faux Louis the Fourteenth table. He had a hand over his mouth and was taking deep breaths, as if to calm his stomach.

"What is it?" I asked.

Doris pointed toward the main room. I lumbered in, cautiously, not sure what to expect. A chocolate pterodactyl hung from the ceiling and flower arrangements that looked vaguely prehistoric stood on every end-table, along with cute little origami triceratops heads. A human-sized tyrannosaurus rex made entirely out of cheese stood on a circular mirror stand in the center of the room. Crock pots filled with chili bubbled on a table leaning against the wall dividing the main room from the bathroom.

"What—?" I started to ask again, and then I saw her.

She was sprawled on the floor, her left hand resting on the glass double doors leading out to the patio. The doors were closed. I cautiously made my way around the cheese dinosaur and the main table, still in the middle of preparations for the night's party, and stopped near her apron-clad torso.

There was no doubt it was Lucinda. She wore a linen pantsuit beneath that apron, and in her right hand she held an apple partially julienned into a stegosaurus. It was her head that was the problem.

It had been stomped flat, crushed into unrecogniz-ability. More gray matter than I would have expected spattered the teal carpet, mixed with more blood than I had ever seen in my life. I swallowed twice, hard, not wanting to repeat the pea soup episode and contaminate the crime scene. Then I cautiously made my way back into the foyer.

"You call the cops?" I asked.

"No!" Doris said. "They'd shut us down."

"Damn straight they'd shut us down," I said. "We have a murderer on the loose here."

The kid moaned and headed toward the bathroom.

I grabbed his arm. "Uh-uh," I said. "Puke in the public restroom. You don't want to contaminate a crime scene."

"Too late," he mumbled, yanked free, and stumbled into the bathroom, kicking the door closed behind him.

"Poor kid," Doris said. "I'm amazed he has any stomach left."

"Listen, Doris, we gotta call the cops." I covered my hand with my sleeve and reached for the black rotary dial on the faux Louis the Fourteenth.

Doris put her hand on mine, forcing the receiver down. "It's Friday afternoon," she said. "Think about what that means."

Eight thousand attendees, all of whom would demand refunds. The hotel, which would sue for breach of contract. The reputation, which would shut down all Los Angeles area conventions for the foreseeable future, not to mention all media cons, not to mention all conventions held in this hotel chain forever.

Millions of dollars, all because Lucinda made someone stomping mad.

"Can't we at least wait until tomorrow?" Doris asked.

Retching sounds echoed from the bathroom. My stomach rolled in sympathy.

"Tomorrow?" I asked. "Don't you remember the party signs that are up all over this convention. For tonight? In this room?"

"Can't we change them to tomorrow night?" she asked. "Then we won't have to refund, and we won't be in breach of contract."

But we would still have the reputation problem, along with another one. "Tampering with a crime scene is illegal, Doris," I said softly.

"Can't you solve this?" she asked. "Can't you solve this before the cops get here?"

"I've never done a murder investigation before, Doris," I said.

"*Please*," she asked. "If we can give them a suspect, they won't shut us down, and Ruth and I can handle the PR problem, at least long enough to save the con."

"You don't care that a woman has been trampled in her own hotel room?"

Doris crossed her muscular arms. "You really need to ask me that, Spade? I wouldn't be so rude as to ask you."

She could have, though. Because I was upset. Lucinda had her points. She made a mean chocolate soufflé, and she knew more about fannish foods than anyone I had ever met. She also had her moments: the charity auction she ran for literacy at Orycon in the early '90s brought in $5,000 more than usual because she browbeat the attendees into spending more money. And she got them to do it by having them buy signed books.

Sometimes I found myself in complete agreement with Lucinda's arguments.

And that terrified me.

I stared at Doris.

"Will you help us?" she asked.

I sighed. "I won't tamper with the crime scene, and I will meet with the police when they arrive. You will call them from this room and you will make sure that no one else enters here. You'll also keep the kid from talking to anyone but me. If I happen to solve this thing before the police arrive, fine. But I won't go any farther than that. I'm not going to let some murderer run loose because you want to hold a media con honoring one of the lamest movies of all time."

"The special effects were cool." The kid had opened the door to the bathroom. He was now a chalk white.

"But the plot sucked," I said. Then I nodded at Doris. "Call. I'm going to snoop a bit. And don't leave until I tell you to. Got that?"

She nodded and reached for the phone. I stopped her. "Cover your hands with your sleeves. And don't touch anything besides that receiver."

She glared at me, but followed my instructions. I prowled into the bedroom, deciding to talk to the kid after his breath cleared up.

Lucinda, not surprisingly, was a neat freak. She had arrived and unpacked, her clothing hanging on her hangers in the walk-in closet. Each item was separated by tissue paper, and her hats were in boxes on the shelf above. Her shoes were lined up below in neat little rows beneath the matching clothes. She had two wigs on the dressing table, one studded with little plastic dinosaurs—the clear brightly colored kind that bartenders used to put in drinks in the mid-sixties. A silver lamé dress hung from the plant hook in the ceiling. Lucinda had planned to go all out on this party, and it surprised me. She had to be doing a favor for someone. Media cons were beneath her—and while she enjoyed fannish cooking, she hated fannish clothing.

I got back into the foyer as Doris hung up the phone. "I didn't tell them it was a murder," she said.

I mentally shook my head. That would be her problem when the cops arrived. It would be better for all of us if I had some idea what had happened.

"Okay, kid," I said to the security boy, "come into my office and talk to me. And don't touch anything."

The kid's color still hadn't returned. He followed me into Lucinda's bedroom and started to close the door.

"Don't touch," I said. We went deep into the bowels of the room, and stopped near the bed. I knew that Doris would have trouble hearing us from this spot because I had had trouble hearing her on the phone.

"What's your name?" I asked.

"Chad," he said. I raised a single eyebrow, Spocklike. I had never met a kid who worked con security named Chad. Or at least, a kid who worked con security who would admit to being named Chad.

"Okay," I said, "I need to know: what made you come to this room in the first place?"

He wiped his mouth with the back of his hand. That stomach of his was amazingly weak. "I was by the flyer table—that was my post—when these fans came down the stairs and told me they'd heard a huge pounding on the fourth floor. They took me to their room on three and I heard it too, like something really heavy was going to crash through the floor. Then I came up here. The door was open, and I let myself in. It was really quiet. I called out to see if anyone was here, and then I saw the food. I went in to grab a snack and—"

He burped, then covered his mouth, swallowing hard. "Sorry," he said.

"It's all right," I said. "Do you know who these fans were?"

"Not by name," he said. "But they have the room be-low this one."

And were probably preparing for another party since the room below also had to be a suite. I rubbed my chin in proper detective fashion. I had a conundrum. I need to talk to those fans, but I didn't want to leave Doris alone in the room. Nor did I want anyone else to know what had happened to Lucinda.

Then I realized it didn't matter. Doris had been in the room without me already. I had investigated, and I knew how things looked. I had seen everything but the bath-room, and that could be remedied.

I took the kid back to the foyer. "Wait here," I said, and peered into the bathroom. The kid had already contami-nated the crime scene—several times—but there didn't seem to be much to see. The bathtub was still maid-spot-less and the counter had Lucinda's make-up and nothing else. The toilet seat was up, one of the towels was askew, and otherwise everything looked fine. It didn't even smell as bad as I thought it would.

"Okay," I said as I emerged. "Let's find those fans. You wait here, Doris, and don't touch anything."

"Don't worry," she said, looking faintly annoyed at the suggestion.

The kid and I slipped into the hallway. The con was fill-ing up. Two women wearing belly dancer skirts and midriff tops, conversed about the proper navel jewel. Five teen-age boys compared tattoos. Three grown men, in Klingon boots and armor, adjusted each other's forehead ridges.

The kid and I took the stairs.

The third floor was filled with people in dinosaur costumes. Some were cheap Halloween masks, while others were full-bore papier-mâché or plastic. The costumes looked heavy, they looked hot, and they smelled of glue. I stared at them, mostly at the feet, wondering what kind of pressure a person would need to drive those hard plastic soles through a skull and crush it.

Then we were in front of 3708. The kid knocked on the door. His hand was shaking.

It was opened by a slender woman whose black hair formed perfect Louisa May Alcott ringlets around her face. She wore a lavender satin shirt with purple satin pants, and the outfit somehow looked perfect on her. Her convention badge was clipped to a tiny piece of cardboard inside her shirt's high pocket, so as not to ruin the satin.

"Hi," she said, looking a bit confused.

"Security," the kid said, glancing at me. "Remember? You asked about the big stomping?"

"Oh, yeah." She was staring at me. Her eyes were lavender, like the shirt. I'd never seen eyes like that in person before. Only in photographs of Elizabeth Taylor. "Who're you?"

"I'm from Ops," I said. "Mind if we come in?"

"Why?" She was asking the kid.

"Because when I went upstairs," he said, "I found—"

I kicked him. He shut up.

"He found that he had a few more questions to ask you," I said. "Mind if we come in."

"No," she said. "I guess not."

She got out of our way, and we stepped into the foyer. It exactly matched the suite above, only here the carpet was brown. Two men sat in the suite's living room. They looked vaguely familiar. They stood as they saw us come in.

"Something wrong?" the first one asked.

He was tall and muscular—those fakey kind of muscles that come from too much health club, and too much low-fat food. His shirt was unbuttoned below the navel, revealing a washboard stomach, and his bare feet looked manicured. His companion wore ripped jeans and a *Star Trek* t-shirt, but unless I missed my guess, his hair had been permed.

Interesting look, for fans. It looked a little too Hollywood, a little too put together, for my tastes. Maybe these folks were slumming.

"You guys with the convention?" I asked.

"What's this all about?" T-Shirt asked. He had his hands on his hips. Same fakey muscles, and he didn't look as if he had ever cracked a book. But, I reminded myself, this was a media con. Folks here didn't have to crack books, even though most of them did.

"Of course we're with the convention," the woman said, and tugged gently on her badge as if to prove it.

"What's your interest?" I asked. "Filking?"

"Excuse me," Manicured asked. His face flamed and he looked insulted.

"Fill-king," the kid said, "not fucking."

Interesting comment, I thought, but I didn't look at him. "Pipe down, Chad," I said. "What are you guys doing at the con?"

"Anyone can come," the woman said, apparently realizing that my questions had more importance than the guys were giving them credit for. "Right?"

"Of course," I said, "but usually people have special reasons for attending. What are yours?"

"We like dinosaurs," T-Shirt said.

"Fascinating," I said in my best Spock voice. No one laughed, even though most fans usually did. My best Spock voice was pretty damn good. "So what's your favorite dinosaur? A plugosaurus or a brontodacdyl?"

"All of 'em," T-Shirt said.

"Hmmm," I said. "Hear you had some noise problems."

"Yeah, man, sounded like weird pounding upstairs," Manicured said. "Like someone was trying to punch a hole in the floor."

"Sounds serious," I said. "Will someone move that chair over here?" I pointed to a square wooden chair that seemed to be the sturdiest thing in the room. T-Shirt moved the chair to the place I pointed to, right next to the balcony doors.

"Spot me, Chad, will you?" I asked as I climbed up.

"Ah, um, ah, you might want me to do that," he said.

"No need," I said, even though the chair was groaning under my weight. I reached up and removed the ceiling panel. Gobs of dust and dirt rained on me, and I had to clear a spider web, but after that I had a pretty good glimpse of the space between the ceiling and the floor above.

"Looks normal," I said, and to my surprise, it did. I put the tile back. "You guys are safe."

"That's it?" the woman asked. "That's all? It sounded wretched up there."

"It was," Chad said. I braced myself on his shoulder and squeezed as I got down. It shut him up again.

"That's it," I said cheerfully. "I hope you have a good con."

"Ah, thanks," T-Shirt said. He was frowning at me.

The kid and I left. The dino costumes flooded the hall. The newer ones looked even more realistic than the earlier ones. Especially the Spielbergian velociraptors. All terrifyingly icky except for the guy wearing blue jeans and a tie-dye brontosaurus head. And the inevitable tot dressed as Barney.

One glance at the elevator told me we weren't going back to the fourth floor that way. Too crowded. It also meant the cops wouldn't come up very quickly when they arrived.

"Where to now?" the kid asked.

I didn't answer. I was feeling pretty annoyed with him. Pretty annoyed with the whole thing, really. I wanted to get back to my Ops computer with its lovely numbers and forget I had ever gotten involved with this detecting business.

Even if I was good at it.

We took the stairs and I was puffing by the time we reached the fourth floor. I hadn't had this much exercise in weeks. And I was moving faster than I liked.

Most of the dino costumes were on the third floor. Regular con-goers littered the fourth. None of them looked like the three ringers downstairs.

I shave-and-a-haircut knocked on 4708. Doris answered immediately. "What took you so long?"

I didn't answer. As I came in, I asked, "Did Lucinda know I was coming to Dinocon?"

"How should I know?" Doris asked.

I glared at her.

She sighed, exasperated. "Probably. If she was looking. You would have been hard to miss since your name was in the con-com listing in all the progress reports. Why?"

I had my suspicions. I made my way back into the suite's main room.

"Hey!" the kid said. "What're you doing?"

His voice had gotten increasingly shrill. I ignored him. I made my way to the body, and, just as I remembered, the floor didn't sag under my considerable weight.

I knelt beside the body. The gray matter and blood were drying in a perfect arch.

"Hey!" the kid yelled. "You said no tampering."

"Grab him, Doris," I said through my teeth. He was getting on my nerves. This whole thing was.

I grabbed the right wrist, dislodging the julienned stegosaurus, and felt—plastic. Soft, lifelike, fake plastic.

"Bitch," I mumbled. I half expected the crushed dummy to mumble "asshole" in return. Then, louder, I said, "Doris, did you call 911?"

She didn't answer. I turned. She was frowning at me. "Doris?"

She flushed. "No," she said. "I called the regular line. I wanted to give you as much time as possible."

Her caution had worked to our advantage. "Call and cancel," I said. "Then break that kid's arm if he doesn't tell you where Lucinda is."

"Lucinda—!"

"Just do it." First time I'd ever understood the sense of a Nike ad.

She twisted the kid's arm up behind his back. Within seconds, he was screaming, "Executive Suite! Executive Suite!"

I got up and walked over to him. "Key," I said.

He handed me a specially marked executive floor key. "Come on, Doris," I said. "Keep a good grip on this kid and commandeer us an elevator."

She did exactly as she was told.

***

ON THE WAY UP, I explained the whole thing, and the kid wisely said nothing, confirming all my suspicions. I was trying to contain my anger, because this thing had just become personal.

And to think I would have mourned the bitch if that had truly been her on the floor below.

You see, the plan was simple: the execution was hard. Lucky for Lucinda that her boyfriend had his new job in Hollywood and even luckier for her that most special effects guys are also sf nerds. Ironic that she needed media people to tamper with a media con. But Lucinda had always been a bit dim when it came to irony.

And, apparently, detail, at least non-food related detail.

First there was the fannish clothing. No matter what kind of theme party Lucinda gave, she never, ever dressed in fannish clothes. No wigs decorated with little plastic dinosaurs, no silver lamé dress. She might have consented to work a media con, but she would never have given up her stylishly proper clothing. She planned the perfect media party, all right, down to the clothes, forgetting that she would never, ever wear those clothes because, of course, she didn't plan to.

But that wasn't the only detail that bothered me. The three "fans" on the floor below had been extras in a straight-to-video sf release that I'd been watching at home a few nights before the con. I would have made them as non-skiffy folk anyway. All science fiction fans—media and lit alike—know the difference between a real dinosaur and a made-up one.

And then there was Chad, clearly another actor for hire. Except he overdid the vomit bit, and the bathroom smelled as if the maid had just left. Lucinda probably hadn't counted on the strength of my sniffer.

But she had counted on me. In fact, I had been the center of her plan. Without me, it wouldn't have worked. She knew that I knew better than to tamper with a crime scene, no matter how great the temptation. She knew that I had a healthy respect for the authorities and that I would insist on cops being present.

And she knew that the cops would see this for the hoax it was. She would appear at the right moment, blame the convention for overreacting to her little party, piss off the cops just enough to get the whole con shut down. The hotel chain would have been angry, the attendees would have demanded refunds, and the whole cascade effect that Doris had foreseen when she first saw that body would have occurred. Media cons, not just in LA, but all over the country would have suffered, and possibly died.

Lucinda's little stunt would have caused more damage than the murder. It was sabotage, served cold.

***

WHEN WE REACHED the executive suite, Doris made the kid open the door. Lucinda saw him, stood up, and cooed. She was dressed for her act in a white sheath that accented her lightly tanned skin and golden hair.

When she saw us, her eyes widened.

"You bitch," Doris said, blowing my line and letting go of the kid. He started to back away, but I shoved him forward and closed the door behind us.

"Back off, Doris," I said. "She's mine. There won't be any cops, Lucinda. You won't ruin this convention."

"I'm going to see that you're banned from cons forever. I'm going to make sure that your name is taken out of the Fannish Directory. I'm going to—"

"For what? For a little party I planned to throw for some friends?" Lucinda asked. "Don't you think it rather cute? I do."

"You—"

Doris lunged for her, and I caught her, staggering a bit under her power. The kid bee-lined for the bathroom, fear making his intentions real this time.

"Go to Ops," I said to Doris. "Tell them everything is fine. I can take it from here."

"I'm going to get you," Doris said, but she listened to me. She knew as well as I did that strange things happened at sf conventions, and that there was no proving malicious intent here.

Knowing about it was something else.

"Misunderstandings are so tragic, Doris," Lucinda said, blinking her blue eyes guilelessly.

Doris growled and disappeared out the door. I stood in front of Lucinda. "Media cons aren't your style."

She smiled. It was sweet as rhubarb pie. "They're not yours either."

"I don't see anything wrong with people having fun. I'm a bit more open-minded than you, Lucinda. I believe people can enjoy reading and watching movies. I believe there's room in fandom for both."

"You're so naive," she said. "These cons are so anti-literature. They appeal only to the ignorant. People who don't understand real science, or real science fiction."

"I think people who think they guard pure science fiction may not understand real science or real science fiction either," I said pointedly.

"Good god," she said, "a philosophical discussion when I have a party to finish."

"It seems strange to me that you'd put on a party here, Lucinda."

She shrugged. "I thought I'd give these people the opportunity to come to a lit-con and see what they were missing."

"So kind of you," I said.

She smoothed her dress. "We all do what we can in the circumstances provided."

At that moment, I almost told her what tripped her up. I almost told her that it was her lack of scientific knowledge, her lack of understanding of forensic science that had destroyed her. First, the splatter had been too pretty, too uniform. Second, and more importantly, the type of force it took to stomp out someone's brains would have caused damage to the plywood floor. Damage someone of my weight would have felt in loose boards or groaning wood.

But I didn't. Why give her the ammunition? She might try again someday.

"Am I excused?" she asked brightly.

"There is no excuse for you, Lucinda," I said in my best fannish manner, and moved out of her way.

***

THE BANE of the non-licensed investigator is that we have no real authority. We can't arrest. Worse yet, people with authority often look down their noses at us.

So we are forced to take some matters into our own hands.

Lucinda, misguided as she was, was clever. Who could prove that the panic the kid, Doris, and I felt was anything more than a product of our own imaginations?

She would say that she had planned a perfect party, and we had nearly ruined it.

In fact, that night, she did carry off the party with full aplomb. She did change the victim from her clone to that of a lawyer, in keeping with *Jurassic Park* (the movie) tradition, and she did pour ice in the bathtub, but those were the only changes she made. The party was the hit of the convention, and became the talk of sf—both media- and literature-oriented—for years to come. It was, in its own way, the Woodstock of science fiction. Eventually everyone who was anyone claimed they had been there, even if they had been clear across the country at the time.

Everyone who was anyone except me.

You see, I was in Ops, checking the computer records. We had an unexplained power failure just as I was transferring Lucinda's credit card information from her con file into an active file so that we could bill her account. Unfortunately, the accident caused blips in her credit record that cascaded down the system and destroyed her credit rating for the next year. She had to defend and deny and repair, all of which took time away from cons and con parties, and fandom.

And somehow she got it in her pretty little head that this would happen again if she ever attempted to sabotage—even accidentally—a major convention again.

Misunderstandings are so tragic.

But we all do what we can in the circumstances provided.

Dragon Slayer

*F*IFTEEN DEAD in less than a century, and not one of them by natural causes. The corpses were always found in some stage of mistreatment, headless being the most common. Occasionally, though, fangs would disappear, and sometimes the right foreleg. Or a wing. And once, just once, the tail.

I collected information on the killings just like I collected sapphires. One corner of my lair was strewn with various death relics—a broadsword, a gauntlet, even a lock of hair found between a victim's back claws.

Something had changed among the humans, something which now made them deadly to dragons.

Fifteen dead in one hundred years was some kind of record. If the killings continued at that rate, we would be extinct within a millennium. Unlike most animals, we didn't breed whenever we glanced at each other. We had rituals, timing, and our own natural infertility working against us.

The infertility concerned the Lair Fathers the most, but it didn't bother me much. It seems logical, if you examine it.

Impregnation takes time—and there's often a year between that event and the laying of the egg.

The lairs themselves are the other problem. We're not social creatures; we don't like to live too close together. Only a few caves are large enough to accommodate one of us. If we wanted to dwell in the same area, we'd have to suffer through rock outcroppings or move into abandoned human dwellings—the large stone kind with towers, poorly built because they crumble after a century or two of neglect.

Still, despite our distance and our solitude, we have our communities, rituals, and ceremonies. Every twenty years, the Lair Fathers hold the governing council. Mostly it is an excuse for everyone in the Five Regions to assemble, catch up on the news, maybe do a little bargaining. But sometimes we have serious business, like the time Vascan's youngest took to looting to increase his hoard.

The youngling was banished to the hinterlands, but apparently didn't survive the trek. The Lair Fathers were called in to look at that corpse, but it was too decayed to determine cause of death. The child could have died of exposure, and been torn apart by animals. Or he could have been murdered and mutilated, like the others.

There was no real way to tell, not without a bit of hair between the claws or a broadsword broken off in the hide.

Failure to determine cause of death didn't make the situation any less of a tragedy, though. The Lair Fathers had to reconsider the punishments they'd established throughout the regions.

The theory being, of course, that punishment didn't teach our people things if no one survived the lessons.

***

WE WERE HEADING into Nae The Loch's Centennial Trade Show and Swap Meet when news of the sixteenth victim hit. Most of us were already in flight—too late to cancel plans even if we'd wanted to.

I didn't want to. I was verging on my first half-millennium, and I was heading to Nae The Loch with more than bargaining on my mind. For the past decade or more, I'd been thinking of adding an egg or two to my stash, and I finally had a large enough hoard to impress a mate.

Females are particular about the places they stash their eggs, a fact I've never understood. Females are never involved with the raising of the hatchlings, preferring to move off to new venues long before the little ones appear. Apparently there is some biological imperative, however, something that makes these flighty creatures particular about egg storage.

Females rarely pick a young male with a small hoard. They seem to prefer males with some experience behind them, and a stash the size of a small mountain.

My father used to say it was because the eggs had to cool under the hoard before hatching—and the bigger the hoard, the safer the egg. But I was never sure of that.

After all, females left eggs all over the countryside. In their fecund period—which can last as long as two millennia—healthy females can drop as many as one hundred eggs, always leaving them in pairs. Rarely do both eggs hatch, and sometimes neither do, but that doesn't negate the sheer irresponsibility of it all.

If females had to feather their nests with food as well as gold, they might not be so quick to abandon their communities.

But to be honest, there isn't a male among us who doesn't envy the female her freedom. All of us wish we could spend our lives exploring the world; we just don't have the wingspan or the stamina to do so.

Besides, we are the only ones who can breathe fire. Until they develop wings of their own, hatchlings require cooked food. It isn't until adolescence that a dragon acquires the ability to eat raw meat without causing serious illness or death.

Most males never acquire a taste for raw food. We prefer to cook our own. Females haven't the time or patience for it. A few of my friends, in their early courting years, tried to seduce a female with a carefully prepared meal of cooked meat, only to have the female turn away in disgust.

I wasn't planning to make that mistake at Nae The Loch. I hoped for a quick courtship, a few months of passion, and then solitude. I wasn't even going to follow the serial seduction plan used by most males so that they would have an egg hoard the size of their jewel hoard. I wanted to take time with my children, and bring one set to adolescence before I risked having another.

Nae The Loch was a good three days flight from my home in Montagneux. Despite the long and difficult flight, I enjoyed Nae The Loch as much as the rest of my people did.

The site was the most protected in the Five Regions. The lake existed inside the highest mountain peak known to dragon. The peak had once been pointed, but several millennia back, steam and pressure broke the peak open, sending boiling lava down the mountainside.

The lava cooled, reinforcing the strength of the exterior mountain, but the inside became something else. Gradually, a lake formed inside the crater. Cool, and deep, and blue—deeper than any lake we had ever encountered—the lake became a courtship destination long before the local males decided to hold the Centennial Swap Meet.

Even though Nae The Loch had a lot of flat land deep within the crater (all of it surrounding the lake), no males could live there. The caves ringing the lake were too small for a proper hoard, but they provided good accommodation for a summer's long trading festival.

Females often stayed in Nae The Loch on their way to other destinations. Rather than drive the females from the area, the Swap Meet brought them. It made meeting males easier, and often prevented difficult encounters on the male's home territory. Too many males fell in love with their mates, and tried to coerce them into staying.

Some females were known to stay for as many as five years. But all were gone long before the eggs began to crack, leaving some males broken-hearted and incapable of proper hatchling care.

As usual, my arrival at Nae The Loch left me breathless, and not just because I rarely flew to such heights. My body could not take more than three days' flight. My wings always ached during the first week of the Swap Meet.

Still, I enjoyed the view as I dove into the crater. Nae The Loch stretched before me as far as I could see. In the center, the lake, a perfect reflection of the pale blue sky. Around it, the black land, covered with flat-top rocks brought centuries ago to serve as tables.

Even from my height, I could see the glitter of gold, the flash of diamonds as the sun struck them. Bits of hoards, no longer wanted, brought for upgrading. I had a few rubies stuck in my pouch. Not a lot, because I couldn't afford much.

At the farthest end of the Swap Meet was the area that interested me. The non-glittery collectibles—a few hand lettered books (I particularly fancied those done in gold leaf); portraits of humans, often framed in gold; and instruments—lutes, pipes, and horns. I fancied a harp one day. At a Swap Meet in La Mer some fifty years before, I had seen one whose frame had been made of gold leaf and whose strings were done in a material strong enough to withstand a small dragon's claws.

Dragons circled the flat area on the longest side of the lake, waiting for their turn to land. All flew at low altitudes so that they couldn't be seen over the mountain peaks.

I joined the throng, bobbing and weaving on the air currents, and trying not to be overwhelmed by the sheer number of my fellows. It sometimes took me as long as a week to be able to handle the crowds, but once I became used to them, I was able to stay for months at a time.

Fortunately, my stash was well hidden, my cave guarded by traps as well as some spells purchased centuries ago from wandering unicorns. I'd allowed nearby vegetation to overgrow the entrance. No one could see the cave but me.

The air up here was thinner, and I had been breathless when I had arrived. I was wheezing after several turns, and I wasn't the only one. The older, heavier males also seemed to have trouble keeping themselves aloft.

One, a grizzled male whose scales had gone from youth's green-gold to age's burnished copper, kept swerving across my flight path. I had to veer sideways twice to avoid hitting him. Finally, his right front claw hooked onto my tail. He didn't pierce the skin, but I lost my balance and would have toppled if two other older males hadn't caught my forearms and held me steady.

"Rumaad?" one of the males said.

I looked up, stunned. I had never been recognized at one of these things before. Most of my friends stayed away, tending their eggs. I was the last of among my peers to think of finding his first mate.

"Yes?" I said, trying not to let my surprise show. Still, I couldn't control the nervous plume of flame that emerged from my left nostril. "Can I be of service?"

"Actually, you can." The dragon who had caught my tail had managed to stop in front of me. He managed a perfect mid-air hover, something few males could accomplish. What had originally seemed like out of control flying must have been his attempts to catch my attention.

I couldn't hover. The males beside me kept me suspended, so that I wouldn't fall to the ground.

"I'm Avagas," the old male said. "I hear you have a stash from the murders."

Avagas. One of the Lair Fathers, a former leader of the Regional Council, and leader of the Rebellion that —three millennia ago— had made the Five Regions the most powerful nation on the Four Continents.

I was embarrassed that he'd heard of my unorthodox collection. I held my breath, trying to hide my shame, but tendrils of smoke slipped between my back teeth anyway.

"I'm not going to chastise you, boy." Avagas sounded faintly amused. "I think your knowledge might be useful."

I took a small breath. His words surprised me. "How?"

"You've heard of the sixteenth victim?"

I had heard at my usual daytime rest stop in the Reed Marsh. The Reed Marsh was deep enough to allow a dragon to submerge himself in mud as protection from the sun, and wide enough to keep his presence a secret from the smaller mammals who would carry the news to the humans.

Four other dragons had chosen the Marsh as their rest stop that day and, as twilight fell and we grew restless, one of the travelers had mentioned the newest death.

"The murder occurred near here. We would like to take you to the body, see what you think of this latest death."

I glanced at the ground below me. I wanted nothing more than to land, lumber into the cave I had reserved at the previous Nae The Loch and nest for a day or two.

But one did not say no to the Lair Fathers, especially one as famous as Avagas.

"I do not know how I can help you," I said.

"You have seen the other bodies, have you not?"

I had no idea how he learned of that. I had visited the other corpses long after the Lair Fathers finished their investigations. The other corpses had been left, according to Five Regions custom, until scavengers had picked the bones clean and a young male, too young to have known the victim, took over the lair.

The hoard would have been scavenged too, but only by family and close friends. By the time I had seen most of the corpses, the only things remaining in their stashes were the imprints the items left in the ground.

"I've seen most of the bodies," I said, because I knew better than to lie. "The early ones were already scattered when I developed my interest."

I didn't tell him though that it was at the early sites where I found the most interesting items—a rusted scabbard picked clean of jewels; rings of metal which I later learned were part of something the humans called chain mail; and a long thin needle coated in ichor.

"Good," Avagas said. "You will come, then?"

"May I rest first?" The shame that had receded rose again. I was tired and this gray eminence, who had lived six times as long as I had, showed no exhaustion at all.

"We shall rest near the corpse," he said. "Come along."

He spun, leaving his place in the landing line, and flew up the cliff face. His companions let go of me, and I bobbled for a moment, before my wings caught the breeze.

It was easier to move forward than it was to try to hover. I managed to keep up with the trio only because one of them would wait for me at each turn.

We went through three passes, all of them part of the peaks that formed Nae The Loch. The passes were narrow and snow-filled, but the chill air felt good to my burning lungs. The flames, which I never controlled well when I was exhausted, shot out unexpectedly twice, once melting snow on the ground below, and once causing a tiny avalanche that tumbled all the way down the mountainside.

From this height, the corpse was easy to spot. It sprawled at tree line, forelegs spread, and tail pointed downhill. The head tilted backwards at an unnatural angle, the unmistakable sign of a broken neck.

As we got closer to the victim, I realized the corpse was unusually large for a male. Then we circled above, and the chill air cooled all the flames in my throat.

The corpse wasn't male at all. It had the silver and black scales of a female in her prime.

Avagas circled and landed on a flat rock far from the corpse. His companions landed beside him, leaving no room for me.

I wasn't going to land beside the corpse. The body rested on snow, and the ground beneath sloped steeply downward. As tired as I was, I might topple, scale over tail, to the forest below.

Instead, I found a second flat rock, some distance from Avagas. I landed harder than I expected, my wings giving out on the descent. I was very out of shape and much too tired. I extended my tongue, stuck the fork into the nearby snow, and shoveled a pile into my mouth.

Cool, refreshing, and much needed. I shoveled another mouthful inside, and felt some of my energy return.

The chill of the mountainside felt good against my scales. I had been overheating as well as exhausting myself. I clambered across the snow, glad that it wasn't that deep here. Otherwise, I would have had to use my wings to keep my weight off the snow, and I didn't think they were up to the task.

I folded them against my back and lumbered toward the corpse.

It looked even bigger up close. Females still scared me—their sheer size was imposing—almost twice the size of males. At first, I stayed back, studying the scene.

Avagas and his companions approached, using their wings to keep themselves slightly above the snow, probably so that the cold wetness wouldn't seep between their claws.

"I told you to look," he called to me while they were still a distance away.

"I am looking," I said. "Stay behind me."

"I do not understand. Why—?"

"Do you want me to find out what happened?"

"We want you to find out how the human reached this height, how close it came to Nae The Loch, and whether or not our most secret place is in danger," Avagas said. "How much time could that take?"

His demands did not surprise me, although he had not stated them before. We had all had the unspoken fear that the humans had found Nae The Loch. It had even been part of the discussion at the Reed Marsh.

"It could take a great deal of time," I said, even though I had never done anything like this before. I had a hunch, though, that the best way to understand what had happened was to study the details.

"What would you have us do?" Avagas asked.

I swiveled my head, trying not to show my surprise. I did not expect him to ask me for instructions.

If I had been with my birth-year companions, I would have given a different answer—a more strident one, which did not take their feelings into account. But, for all his interest, Avagas was a Lair Father. I could not order him about like an equal.

"Perhaps," I said, "it would be best if your companions brought us the evening meal. I have been flying all day, and I'm sure this crisis has occupied you. We shall be here for some time. Nourishment would be advised."

Avagas waved a claw, not even bothering to repeat my words. The other two males flew off.

"And me?" Avagas asked.

"Observe," I said. "Between the two of us, we might decipher what happened here."

The snow around the corpse was littered with small holes. The corpse had hit hard, sending ice chunks and debris into the air. They landed in a splatter pattern around the body.

126

"Your caution amazes me," Avagas said. "I would simply like to find the human source of our troubles and slay him before he makes our situation worse."

His words startled me away from my examination. Did he know nothing of humans? "It is not one human who has been killing our people. Humans live six or seven decades at most. Toward the end, they are frail creatures, not even worthy of a hatchling snack."

His head tilted, revealing the tender underside of his jaw line. "Then what is this killing? I cannot believe it accidental."

"It is not. I believe the humans have a ritual, which requires proof of dragon slaying," I said. "Perhaps the Lair Fathers should capture a young human and quiz him about their customs."

"We cannot speak to those beasts," Avagas said. "They do not know the holy tongue."

"But they have their own tongue. It is fine and rich. I'm sure one of us speaks it."

"Besides you?" Avagas swiveled his head back so that he stared at the corpse.

"I do not speak it," I said, trying not to let him hear the regret in my voice. I often wished I had spoken it, so that I would understand the texts I'd found, the songs I'd heard. "But there are traders at the Swap Meet who do."

Avagas sighed, as if speaking the human tongue were a thing beneath dragons. He did not say another word, and I flattered myself that he was considering the suggestion.

I examined each hole in the snow, realizing in short order that my first assumption about them had been right. I waddled closer to the corpse until I stood over it.

Because the death had been a recent one, and because the temperature on this mountainside was chill, the corpse had been preserved as if in life. Her eyes were closed and if one ignored the angle of her head, it would appear as if she had just fallen asleep in the snow.

She had been a magnificent creature. She had a long, narrow snout, and sharp teeth that rose above her upper lip. Her talons were scraped to fine points, and the ridges along her spine nearly hid a band of well-developed muscle that ran along her ribcage.

Her wings were still partly extended. They were thin as flower petals and probably were that soft to the touch. The silver-black of her scales had a touch of green, making them seem almost iridescent. Her tail was thick and powerful, the barb on the end intact and free of blood.

She had not attacked anyone.

I stepped closer, careful where I put my hind feet. I knew that my tail would obliterate any marks in the snow, and I made certain I examined them before I destroyed them.

So far the marks had told me little.

Avagas watched me, as if I were the curiosity, not the dead female. When I reached the weapons embedded in her side, he finally sighed, a bit of flame leaking through his nose.

Apparently I had finally reached the part of the body he had wanted me to see.

Three projectile weapons lodged in her back flank. The weapons were short and stubby, feathered on the ends. I had seen their like before, often littered around lairs. Humans who hunted dragons with these weapons—which they called arrows—often became lunch.

There were longer versions of the arrow, more effective versions—some as tall as the human who wielded them. These weapons, called spears, could slip beneath scales, go between ribs, and find a dragon's heart.

The arrows, small as they were, rarely pierced skin.

The tips of these arrows had gotten caught between the larger scales of the female's back. I doubted she even felt them. The feathers were wind-torn and had been sheered off one of the weapons.

She'd been carrying the arrows for some time. No one had bothered to tell her of them or help her remove them. Someone probably would have noticed at Nae The Loch, and helped her there.

It might have been the beginning of a beautiful courtship.

"Human weapons," Avagas said. "They are more destructive than we thought."

"These weapons could not have disturbed her flight," I said. "She took them on the ground. Notice the angle of entry. Whoever shot them hit her from above, not below."

Avagas crept beside me. I glanced at the snow in his path, and saw nothing that would be disturbed by his presence.

"I had not thought of that," he muttered. "Yet she has clearly fallen from the sky."

"Something brought her down," I said. "I have a theory, but I am unwilling to discuss it until I examine her more closely."

I walked around the corpse. Mine were the only footprints near the body. The tiny holes from the dirt and ice surrounded the corpse, adding to my theory that she had dropped mid-flight.

Then I realized why that disturbed me. A dragon whose flight was broken did not drop like a stone from the air. A dragon, particularly one with a wingspan as magnificent as this female's, would glide until she saw a proper spot, and land on it.

Even if she were forced to land in a place like this, she would have brought herself in, hind feet first, scraping to slow her approach if she had to, tail as ballast, until she came to a stop.

Instead, she had landed on her belly like a flopping fish.

I walked around her other side. Finally, I saw fresh damage. Many of her scales had been ripped off. Slashes cut deep into her flesh, and blood stained the remaining scales, covering their lovely silver-green finish.

I followed the twisted neck to the head and peered at it again. She had a white patch of scales between her ear bumps. I'd seen a patch like that once before, a hundred years ago.

She'd been at Nae The Loch both times I'd been here, each time prowling for a mate. Her name was Paeche. The last time I'd seen her, she'd bent her head toward me, butted me in the side, and said, *I like a male whose neck still bears a touch of red. Have you mated yet, youngling? Would you like to learn the ways of dragons?*

Her approach had terrified me, and I had moved away from her, to the amusement of the traders at their tables. One of the traders later confided in me that Paeche liked her males young and biddable, and it was best that I had not become involved with her, because I would expect an attachment, and she often left the pairing without laying a single egg.

It had been that moment with her that had put me off my quest for a mate at the last Nae The Loch, convincing me that I still had much to learn about females. That did not stop my friends from becoming her conquests. Two of my birth-year companions had heeded her invitation, only to become locked in a struggle over mating rights.

She left both of them for a male I had not met, a son of one of the table traders, who abandoned the Swap Meet altogether and took her to his lair.

"What do you see?" Avagas asked. Apparently my analysis of the human weapons had impressed him. He seemed to have more patience than he'd had earlier.

I did not tell him I recognized the female. I made myself look away from the white patch. More scrapes ran along the side and back of her skull. The scrapes were deep, and at the edges, puncture marks.

Four of them, as I had expected.

Avagas' companions flew overhead, their wings whistling in the wind. In their foreclaws, they each carried an iron container. The meal that I had requested.

They flew past, and Avagas headed toward them. He probably expected me to follow, but I was unwilling.

The light was dimming, and I wanted to see one last thing before the sun set over the mountain peaks. I peered closely at the scales running along the right side of Paeche's face.

Scorch marks ran down the center of her shapely snout. I didn't have to sniff them to know they would smell faintly of sulfur.

I sat down in the snow, feeling even more tired than I had when I'd arrived.

Humans did not slay this dragon. Instead, she had been murdered by one of our own.

***

AVAGAS INSISTED on a full explanation of my theory. We sat around the fire we'd started with the wood the companions had gathered, and snacked from the iron containers. Raw meat—mostly animal flesh—had been piled inside. We each speared a piece with our claws, charred it with our own breath, and ate long into the night.

The corpse had given up details so clear that I could almost imagine the murder.

Whoever had attacked Paeche had known her flight path and had waited for her on a nearby peak. I knew that if we flew the surrounding peaks at dawn, we'd find the imprint of a small dragon's tail and hindquarters in the otherwise pristine snow.

Paeche's killer had waited for her, and when he saw her, he crouched until she passed. Then he flew after her.

He was small enough to slip between her wings, but the strategy didn't work as well as he thought. She must have caught him, making him tumble away from her. As he spun in the air, his back claws dug into her side, ripping it open, and angering her.

She turned on him, but he surprised her with a blast of fire across the snout.

As she pawed at her eyes, perhaps trying to protect them from the flames, he flew above her, and grabbed her skull with his forelegs, puncturing through the scales and skin with his claws.

Either she turned or he yanked or both. Ultimately, it did not matter. The movement—its suddenness and ferocity—killed her.

She dropped like a stone from the sky, and he fled—whether in fear or triumph, I could not tell.

After my fifth retelling in which I explained how her impact had caused the snow to rain around her corpse all at the same time, after I had again detailed the difference between fresh wounds and older ones, after I had explained how arrows (as opposed to their larger cousins, spears) could not kill a female dragon, Avagas was finally satisfied with my interpretation.

We both knew he would investigate for himself come dawn, but that did not disturb me. In his place, I would have done the same.

What disturbed me, and what I did not say, was that we had no punishments for dragon-upon-dragon slayings. Such things were unheard of. Because we were solitary creatures who rarely interacted, we did not solve our differences through killings.

Certainly, we neglected our eggs at times, but eggs were not hatchlings. Once a hatchling took its first breath, it became a dragon, subject to all the respect accorded to one of our kind.

Respect Paeche had not.

***

I woke before dawn to find Avagas stoking the fire with more wood, then blasting it into a bonfire with a single breath of flame. His eyes were red-rimmed, his scales even grayer than they had seemed in the daylight.

He had not slept at all. It was clear this matter disturbed him as much as it disturbed me.

His companions snored, curled around the iron containers as if they were a stash instead of boxes that had to be returned to some trading table.

Sleeping in the snow left me sluggish. Cold had never agreed with me. I did not appreciate the slower heart rate, and the feeling that, if I stayed but a day or two longer, I would become a block of ice.

I sat up, and Avagas handed me a piece of meat so charred that it crunched as I ate it. I washed it down with some melted snow.

When he finally spoke, it was with weary resignation. "Nothing in your details gives us any hint as to who did this. All we know is that our culprit is male."

I licked the last of the burned meat off my claws, considering my response. If I told him what I had dreamed of, we would move from the realm of certainty to the realm of conjecture. I was not certain that conjecture was appropriate.

He sent another blast of flame at the fire, although it did not need stoking.

"I almost wish it had been a human after all," he said softly. "At least then, I would know what to do."

He was right. Our options in that case were plentiful. We could defend Nae The Loch with young males or abandon the site altogether. If neither of those plans satisfied the Lair Fathers and the rest of the Five Regions, we might terrorize the humans, setting fire to nearby cities and driving them from the area.

Driving humans away did not last, but the humans who would return to a settlement decades later did not seem to be related to the group who had fled there. Such an action would have a good chance of preserving Nae The Loch.

"What of the other Lair Fathers?" I asked. "Perhaps they—?"

"No." Avagas' tone was pained. "I am one of the few who remembers the Rebellion. It is the last time that dragon turned on dragon."

"That we know of."

He swiveled his head toward me. "What do you mean?"

I could not look at him as I spoke. "For the most part, we live alone and die alone. Often our corpses are not discovered for decades. Who is to say that a dragon was murdered? It cannot be proven after so long a time. We were fortunate to find this female so quickly after her death—and even more fortunate that we investigated. If we had not, we might have thought that she had landed wrong, breaking her neck, or—if enough time had passed—we might have found only the tips of the human weapons, and concluded that a human had killed her after all."

Smoke curled from his nostrils. Avagas looked as if he wanted to blast the fire again, but he could not. There wasn't enough wood left to take the brunt of the flames. He would risk burning his sleeping friends.

"So the fifteen—"

"May have died at human hands," I said.

"May." A small puff of smoke followed the word out of his mouth.

"I have often thought it curious that creatures who wear armor that clanks and carry weapons that can rarely slice through our scales have managed to slay fifteen of us," I said.

Avagas bowed his head.

He did not seem to want to hear what I had to say, but now that I had started, I had to continue. "I do know that at least one of the fifteen died from a human-inflicted wound. I once found a needle covered in ichor."

Ichor was only found in a dragon's eye. An eye without ichor was concave, and the dragon blind.

"I believe a human found his victim napping, crept on top of the victim's head and pierced his eye before the victim even realized he was under attack. A dragon in such pain would thrash, but not be able to harm something so small, clinging to his skull."

Avagas wrapped his tail around his hindquarters, head still down, obviously listening.

"It would take little to blind the other eye, and then the dragon would be helpless. A human in such a position could find the tender spot beneath the jaw, shove a sword into it, severing the fire pipes and the lungs. It would take time, but in that circumstance, any one of us would die."

"But what of the others? The mutilations? We had always thought they were caused by humans." Avagas spoke so softly I could barely hear him above the snores.

"So they were." The cold had gotten worse. I leaned closer to the fire. "But there is no way to know when these mutilations occurred. Perhaps they occurred long after death, and the human returned to his tribe, regaling them with his exploits when in truth all he had done was slice a part from a corpse."

"Your theories make sense." Avagas shuddered. "I do not like them."

This, then, was my chance to discuss the last one. Still, I hesitated, knowing if I did, all that we understood about dragon custom would change.

"Then let me give you one more," I said.

He closed his eyes, as if he did not want to hear. Then he sighed, and opened them. "Speak."

"This is not a common path to Nae The Loch. I doubt many males travel this distance. There is little food in the snow and there are no obvious resting areas. Females may go this route, but in this case, we must not concern ourselves with females."

The snoring stopped, and so did I. Then the nearest companion huddled closer to his iron chest, and let out a whistling breath. The other companion grunted. Their snores rose in harmony once again.

I lowered my voice. "If the male who first reported seeing her corpse is also a male who has mated with her, then you will probably have your killer."

"Why?" Avagas asked.

"He would know her flight path, and he would—"

"I meant," Avagas said, "what would cause anyone to attack a female? Let us forget that she is larger and more powerful. Females are not a permanent part of our lives. There is no reason to destroy them."

"Males get irrational about their mates," I said. "And Paeche was known for consummating but rarely completing the cycle. This killer had the advantage. He had surprise on his side. Yet he chose to burn her face instead diving beneath her and going for the tender spot."

"And this has given you a theory?"

I poked the fire with one claw. "I believe that our killer was trying to get her to return to his lair, to finish something they had begun a century ago. He did not mean to kill her. Instead, he meant to use flame to force her to fly away with him."

"For that to work," Avagas said, "he would have to have a lair near here."

"And not many do," I said. "It would seem that you have but to look through Nae The Loch. The killer should not be hard to find."

***

AND INDEED, he was not. As I suspected, the killer was the trader's son who had lured Paeche to his lair at the last Swap Meet. She left while he slept one night, without a word. There were no eggs, nothing to remember her by, except the humiliation of an improperly completed mating.

He had a century to plan how to get her to return.

When confronted, he confessed to the murder. It had happened as I had imagined it—an accident in the midst of a badly made plan.

The Lair Fathers are debating his punishment now. Some want to reinstate banishment. Others disagree, believing it is not harsh enough. A few have suggested leaving him to the females.

Throughout this all, he has been imprisoned in a shallow cave at the mouth of Nae The Loch, guarded by males with more fire power than the rest of us combined.

What becomes of him does not concern me. I am not a Lair Father, and probably not destined to be one.

My concerns are new, things I had never considered before. And because of them, I find myself in a strange position.

My collection of relics from the fifteen deaths, once considered esoteric and slightly odd, has made me famous in the Five Regions. There is talk that I should investigate all new deaths as soon as we learn of them.

I do not like this idea. It requires travel, and I know of no way it will help me improve my own stash. And I need to concentrate on my hoard since I did not find a mate at Nae The Loch.

Indeed, the females abandoned the place when they learned of the murders. There is talk that the females will not return to the Swap Meet. Instead, they will flock to other festivals, ones in less remote locations.

Because of one male's actions, females now view all of us with suspicion.

Still, I think back to that moment on the snow-covered mountainside, as I realized the corpse left me a message about her death.

All males collect. Our hoards are what separate us from each other. Anyone can find sapphires or diamonds. Most of us have, at one point or another, raided human dwellings for gold.

But I am the only dragon in recorded history—male or female—who has collected information and, more to the point, the only one who has found value in it.

I like that distinction. But the distinction also disturbs me. Because, for my collection to maintain its value, the information must remain useful.

I am not certain I want to read corpses. I do not think I will like what they tell me.

I have reviewed my collection, looked over the items found at the fifteen death sites. Only the needle contains a substance from a dragon's body.

The other items carry human blood or bones too tiny to be dragon. It seems to me that the humans died at the whims of a dragon, as they always have, and only once was it the other way around.

Which means that fourteen male dragons died before their time.

We are large creatures, with no natural predators. We should all die of ill health or old age. Yet fourteen of us were murdered—in the space of a very short time.

Something has changed in the past century. Initially, we thought it was the humans.

Now we know it is not.

What frightens me the most about this is that the details show me one other thing, something I have confided in no one else.

It is true that the fourteen died at another dragon's hand. However, I do not believe that a single dragon committed the killings.

I believe we as a species have changed. And it is clear that change could doom us all.

The Retrieval Artist

I HAD JUST COME OFF a difficult case, and the last thing I wanted was another client. To be honest, not wanting another client is a constant state for me. Miles Flint, the reluctant Retrieval Artist. I work harder than anyone else in the business at discouraging my clients from seeking out the Disappeared. Sometimes the discouragement fails and I get paid a lot of money for putting a lot of lives in danger, and maybe, just maybe, bringing someone home who wants to come. Those are the moments I live for, the moments when it becomes clear to a Disappeared that home is a safe place once more.

Usually though, my clients and their lost ones are more trouble than they're worth. Usually, I won't take their cases for any price, no matter how high.

I do everything I can to prevent client contact from the start. The clients who approach me are the courageous ones or the really desperate ones or the ones who want to use me to further their own ends.

I try not to take my cases personally. My clients and their lost ones depend on my objectivity. But every once in a while, a case slips under my defenses—and never in the way I expect.

This was one of those cases. And it haunts me still.

2

MY OFFICE is one of the ugliest dives on the Moon. I found an original building still made of colonial permaplastic in the oldest section of Armstrong, the Moon's oldest colony. The dome here is also made of permaplastic, the clear kind, although time and wear have turned it opaque. Dirt covers the dome near the street level. The filtration system tries to clean as best it can, but ever since some well-meaning dome governor pulled the permaplastic flooring and forgot to replace it, this part of Armstrong Dome has had a dust problem. The filtration systems have been upgraded twice in my lifetime, and rebuilt at least three times since the original settlement, but they still function at one-tenth the level of the state-of-the-art systems in colonies like Gagarin Dome and Glenn Station. Terrans newly off the shuttle rarely come to this part of Armstrong; the high-speed trains don't run here, and the unpaved streets strike most Terrans as unsanitary, which they probably are.

The building that houses my office had been the original retail center of Armstrong, or so says the bronze plaque that someone had attached to the plastic between my door and the rent-a-lawyer's beside me. We are an historic building, not that anyone seems to care, and rent-a-lawyer once talked to me about getting the designation changed so that we could upgrade the facilities.

I didn't tell him that if the designation changed, I would move.

You see, I like the seedy look, the way my door hangs slightly crookedly in its frame. It's deceptive. A careless Tracker would think I'm broke, or equally careless. Most folks don't guess that the security in my little eight-by-eight cube is state of the art. They walk in, and they see permaplastic, and a desk that cants slightly to the right, and only one chair behind it. They don't see the recessed doors that hide my storage in the wall between the rent-a-lawyer's cube and my own, and they don't see the electronics because they aren't looking for them.

I like to keep the office empty. I own an apartment in one of Armstrong's better neighborhoods. There I keep all the things I don't care about. Things I do care about stay in my ship, a customized space yacht named *The Emmeline*. She's my only friend and I treat her like a lover. She's saved my life more times than I care to think about, and for that (and a few other things), she deserves only the best.

I can afford to give her the best, and I don't need any more work although, as I said, I sometimes take it. The cases that catch me are usually the ones that catch me in my Sir Galahad fantasy—the one where I see myself as a rescuer of all things worthy of rescue—although I've been known to take cases for other reasons.

But, as I'd said, I'd just come off a difficult case, and the last thing I needed was another client. Especially one as young and innocent as this one appeared to be.

She showed up at my door wearing a dress, which no one wears in this part of Armstrong any more, and regular shoes, which had to have been painful to walk in. She also had a personal items bag around her wrist, which, in this part of town, was like wearing a giant *Mug Me!* sign. The bags were issued on shuttles and only to passengers who had no idea about the luggage limitations.

She was tall and raw-boned, but slender, as if diet and exercise had reduced her natural tendency toward lushness. Her dress, an open and inexpensive weave, accented her figure in an almost unconscious way. Her features were strong and bold, her eyes dark, and her hair even darker.

My alarm system warned me she was outside, staring at the door or the plaque or both. A small screen popped up on my desk revealing her and the street beyond. I shut off the door alarm, and waited until she knocked. Her clutched fist, adorned with computer and security enhancements that winked like diamonds in the dome's fake daylight, rapped softly on the permaplastic. The daintiness of the movement startled me. I wouldn't have thought her a dainty woman.

I had been cleaning up the final reports, notations and billings from the last case. I closed the file and the keyboard (I never use voice commands for work in my office—too easily overheard) folded itself into the desk. Then I leaned back in the chair, and waited.

She knocked three times, before she tried the door. It opened, just like it had been programmed to do in instances like this.

"Mr. Flint?" Her voice was soft, her English tinted with a faintly Northern European accent.

I still didn't say anything. She had the right building and the right name. I would wait to see if she was the right kind of client.

She squinted at me. I was never what clients expected. They expected a man as seedy as the office, maybe one or two unrepaired scars, a face toughened by a hard life and space travel. Even though I was thirty-five, I still had a look some cultures called angelic: blond curls, blue eyes, a round and cherubic face. A client once told me I looked like the pre-Raphaelite paintings of Cupid. I had smiled at him and said, *Only when I want to.*

"Are you Mr. Flint?" The girl stepped inside, then slapped her left hand over the enhancements on her right. She looked faintly startled, as if someone had shouted in her ear.

Actually, my security system had cut in. Those enhancements linked her to someone or something outside herself, and my system automatically severed such links, even if they had been billed as unseverable.

"You want to stay in here," I said, "you stay in here alone. No recording, no viewing, and no off-site monitoring."

She swallowed, and took another step inside. She was playing at being timid. The real timid ones, severed from their security blankets, bolt.

"What do you want?" I asked.

She flinched, and took another step forward. "I understand that you—find—people."

"Where did you hear that?"

"I was told in New York." One more step and she was standing in front of my desk. She smelled faintly of lavender soap mixed with nervous sweat. She must have come here directly from the shuttle. A woman with a mission, then.

"New York?" I asked as if I'd never heard of it.

"New York City."

I had several contacts in New York, and a handful of former clients. Anyone could have told her, although none were supposed to. They always did though; they always saw their own desperation in another's eyes, figured it was time to help, time to give back whatever it was they felt they had gained.

I sighed. "Close the door."

She licked her lips—the dye on them was either waterproof or permanent—and then walked back to the door. She looked into the street as if she would find help there, then gently pushed the door closed.

I felt a faint hum through my wrist as my computer notified me that it had turned the door security back on.

"What do you want?" I asked before she turned around.

"My mother," she said. "She's—"

"That's enough." I kept my tone harsh, and I didn't stand. I didn't want this girl/woman to be too comfortable. It was always best to keep potential clients off balance.

Children, young adults, and the elderly were the obvious choices of someone trying to use my system for the wrong purposes, and yet they were the ones most likely to contact me. They never seemed to understand the hostility I had to show clients, the insistence I put on identity checks, and they always balked at the cost. *It feels as if I'm on trial, Mr. Flint*, they would say, and I wouldn't respond. They were. They had to be. I always had to be sure they were only acting on their own interests. It was too easy for a Tracker to hire someone to play off a Retrieval Artist's sympathies, and initiate a search that would get the Disappeared killed—or worse.

The girl turned. Her body was so rigid that it looked as if I could break her in half.

"I don't find people," I said. "I uncover them. There's a vast difference. If you don't understand that, then you don't belong here."

That line usually caused half my potential clients to exit. The next line usually made most of the remaining fifty percent excuse themselves, never to darken my door again.

"I charge a minimum of two million credits, Moon issue, not Earth issue—" which meant that they were worth triple what she was used to paying—"and I can charge as much as ten million or more. There is no upper limit on my costs nor is there one on my charges. I charge by the day, with expenses added in. Some investigations take a week, some take five years. You would be my exclusive employer for the period of time it takes to find your—mother—or whomever I'd be looking for. I have a contract. Several of my former clients have tried to have the courts nullify it. It holds up beautifully. I do not take charity cases, no matter what your sob story is, and I do not allow anyone to defer payment. The minute the money stops, so do I."

She threaded her fingers together. Her personal items bag bumped against her hip as she did so. "I'd heard about your financial requirements." Which meant that one of my former clients had recommended me to her. Dammit. "I have limited funds, but I can afford a minor investigation."

I stood. "We're done talking. Sorry I can't help you." I walked past her and pulled open the door. Security didn't mind if I did that. It would have minded if she had.

"Can't you do a limited search, Mr. Flint?" Her eyes were wide and brown. If she was twenty, she was older than I thought. I checked for tears. There were none. She could be legit, and for that I was sorry.

I closed the door so hard the plastic office shook. "Here's what you're asking me," I said. "If the money runs out, I quit searching, which is no skin off my nose. But I'll have dug a trail up to that particular point, and your mother—or whomever I'm looking for—"

She flinched again as I said that. A tender one. Or a good actress.

"—would be at more of a risk than she is now. Right now, she's simply disappeared. And since you've come to me, you've done enough research to know that one of six government programs—or one of fifteen private corporations—have gone to considerable expense to give her a new life somewhere else. If the cover on that existence gets blown, your mother dies. It's that simple. And maybe, just maybe, the people who helped her will die too, or the people who are now important to her, or the people who were hidden with her, for whatever reason. Half an investigation is a death sentence. Hell, sometimes a full investigation is a death sentence. So I don't do this work on whim, and I certainly don't do it in a limited fashion. Are we clear?"

She nodded, just once, a rabbit-like movement that let me know I'd connected.

"Good," I said and pulled the door back open. "Now get out."

She scurried past me as if she thought I might physically assault her, and then she hurried down the street. The moon dust rose around her, clinging to her legs and her impractical dress, leaving a trail behind her that was so visible, it looked as if someone were marking her as a future target.

I closed the door, had the security system take her prints and DNA sample off the jamb just in case I needed to identify her someday, and then tried not to think of her again.

It wouldn't be easy. Clients were rare and, if they were legit, they always had an agenda. By the time they found me, they were desperate, and there was still a part of me that was human enough to feel sympathy for that.

Sympathy is rare among Retrieval Artists. Most Retrieval Artists got into this line of work because they owed a favor to the Disty, a group of aliens who'd more or less taken over Mars. Others got into it because they had discovered, by accident, that they were good at it, usually making that discovery in their jobs for human corporations or human crime syndicates.

I got in through a different kind of accident. Once I'd been a space cop assigned to Moon Sector. A lot of the Disappeared come through here on their way to new lives, and over time, I found myself working against a clock, trying to save people I'd never met from the people they were hiding from. The space police frowned on the work—the Disappeared are often reformed criminals and not worth the time, at least according to the Moon Sector—and so, after one of the most horrible incidents of my life, I went into business on my own.

I'm at the top of my profession, rich beyond all measure, and usually content with that. I chose not to have a spouse or children, and my family is long-dead, which I actually consider to be a good thing. Families in this business are a liability. So are close friends. Anyone who can be broken to force you to talk. I don't mind being alone.

But I do hate to be manipulated, and I hate even more to take revenge, mine or anyone else's. I vigilantly protect myself against both of those things.

And this was the first time I failed.

3

AFTER THE GIRL LEFT, I stayed away from the office for two days. Sometimes snubbed clients come back. They tell me their stories, the reasons they're searching for their parent/child/spouse, and they expect me to understand. Sometimes they claim they've found more money. Sometimes they simply try to cry on my shoulder, believing I will sympathize.

Once upon a time maybe I would have. But Sir Galahad has calluses growing on his heart. I am beginning to hate the individuals. They always take a level of judgment that drains me. The lawyers trying to find a long-lost soul to meet the terms of a will; the insurance agents, required by law to find the beneficiaries, forced by the government to search "as far as humanly possible without spending the benefits"; the detective, using government funds to find the one person who could put a career criminal, serial killer, or child molester, away for life; these people are the clients I like the most. Almost all are repeat customers. I still have to do background checks, but I have my gut to rely on as well. With individuals, I can never go by gut, and even armed with information, I've been burned.

I've gotten to the point where coldness is the way of the game for me, at least at first. Once I sign on, I become the most intense defender of the Disappeared. The object of my search also becomes the person I protect and care about the most. It takes a lot of effort to maintain that caring, and even more to manage the protection.

Sometimes I'll go to extremes.

Sometimes I have no other choice.

On the third day, I went back to my office, and of course, the girl was waiting. This time she was dressed appropriately, a pair of boots, cargo pants that cinched at the ankles, and a shirt the color of sand. Her personal items bag was gone—obviously someone, probably the maître d' at the exclusive hotel she was most likely staying at, told her it made her a mark for pickpockets and other thieves. Thin mesh gloves covered her enhancements. Only her long hair marked her as a newcomer. If she stayed longer than a month, she'd cut it off just like the rest of us rather than worry about keeping it clean.

She was leaning against my locked door, her boot-ed feet sticking into the street. In that outfit, she looked strong and healthy, as if she were hiring me to take her on one of those expeditions outside the dome. The rent-a-lawyer next door, newly out of Armstrong Law, was eye-ing her out of his scarred plastic window, a sour expression on his thin face. He probably thought she was scaring away business.

I stopped in the middle of the street. It was hot and airless as usual. There was no wind in the dome, of course, and the recycled air got stale real fast. Half the equipment in this part of town had been on the fritz for the last week, and the air here wasn't just stale, it was thin and damn near rancid. I hated breathing bad air. The shallow breaths, and the increased heartbeat made me feel as if there was danger around when there probably wasn't. If the air got any thinner, I'd have to start worrying about my clarity of thought.

She saw me when I was still several meters from the place. She stood, brushed the dust off her pants, and watched me. I pretended as if I were undecided about my next move, even though I knew I'd have to confront her sooner or later. Her kind only went away when chased.

"I'm sorry," she said as I approached. "I was told that you expected negotiation, so I—"

"Lied about the money, did you?" I asked, knowing she was lying now too. If she knew enough to find me, she also knew that I didn't negotiate. All the lie proved was that she had an ego big enough to believe that the rules were different for her.

I shoved past her to use my palm to unlock the door. I only used a palm scan when someone else was present. It let us in, but initiated a higher level of security monitoring.

She started to follow me, but I slammed the door in her face. Then I went to my desk, and switched on my own automatic air. It was illegal, and it wouldn't be enough, but I wasn't planning to stay long. I would finish the reports from the last case, get the final fees, and then maybe I'd take a vacation. I had never taken one before. It was past time.

I wish, now, that I had listened to my gut and gone. But there was just enough of Sir Galahad left in me to make me watch the door. And of course, it opened just like I expected it to.

She came inside, a little downtrodden but not defeated. Her kind seldom were. "My name is Anetka Sobol," she said as if I should know it. I didn't. "I really do need your help."

"You should have thought of that before," I said. "This isn't a game."

"I'm not trying to play one."

"So what was that attempt at negotiation?"

She shook her head. "My source—"

"Who is your source?"

"He said I wasn't—"

"Who is it?"

Again she licked that lower lip just like she had the day before, a movement that was too unconscious to be planned. The nervousness, then, wasn't feigned. "Norris Gonnot."

Gonnot. Sobol was the third client he'd sent to me in the last year. The other two checked out, and both cases had been easy to solve. But he was making himself too visible, and I would have to deal with that, even though I hated to do so. He was extremely grateful that I had found his daughter and granddaughter alive (although they hadn't appreciated it), and he'd been even more grateful when I was able to prove that the Disty were no longer looking for them.

"And how did you find him?"

She frowned. "Does it matter?"

I leaned back in my chair. It squeaked and the sound made her jump ever so slightly. "Either you're up front with me now or the conversation ends."

The frown grew deeper, and she clutched her left wrist with her right hand, holding the whole mess against her stomach. The gesture looked calculated. "Do you treat everyone like this?"

"Nope. Some people I treat worse."

"Then how do you get any work?"

I shrugged. "Just lucky."

She stared at me for a moment. Then she glanced at the door. Was she letting her thoughts be that visible on purpose or was she again acting for my benefit? I wasn't sure.

"A cop told me about him. Norris, that is." She sounded reluctant. "I wasn't supposed to tell you."

"Of course not. Gonnot wasn't supposed to talk to anyone. This cop, was he a rent-a-cop, a real cop, a Federal cop, or with the Earth Force?"

"She," she said.

"Okay," I said. "Was she a—"

"She was a New York City police officer who had her own detective agency."

"That's illegal in New York."

She shrugged. "So?"

I closed my eyes. Ethics had disappeared everywhere. "You hired her?"

"She was my fifth private detective. Most would work for a week and then quit when they realized that searching for an interstellar Disappeared is a lot harder than finding a missing person."

I waited. I'd heard that sob story before. Most detectives kept the case and simply came to someone like me.

"Of course," she said, "my father's looming presence doesn't help either."

"Your father?"

She was staring at me as if I had just asked her what God was.

"I'm Anetka Sobol," she said as if that clarified everything.

"And I'm Miles Flint. My name doesn't tell you a damn thing about my father."

"My father is the founding partner of the Third Dynasty."

I had to work to hide my surprise. I knew what the Third Dynasty was, but I didn't know the names of its founders. The Dynasty itself was a formidable presence all over the galaxy. It was a megacorp with its fingers in a lot of pies, mostly to do with space exploration, establishing colonies in mineral rich areas, and exploitation of new resources. My contacts with the Third Dynasty weren't on the exploration level, but within its narrow interior holdings. The Third Dynasty was the parent company for Privacy Unlimited, one of the services which helped people disappear.

Privacy Unlimited had been developed, as so many of the corporate disappearance programs had, when humans discovered the Disty, and realized that in some alien cultures, there was no such word as forgiveness. The Disty were the harshest of our allies. The Revs, the Wygnin, and the Fuetrer also targeted certain humans, and our treaties with these groups allowed the targeting if the aliens could show cause.

The balance was a delicate one, allowing them their cultural traditions while protecting our own. Showing cause had to happen before one of eighteen multicultural tribunals, and if one of those tribunals ruled in the aliens' favor, the humans involved were as good as dead. We looked the other way most of the time. Most of the lives involved were, according to our government, trivial ones. But of course, those people whose lives had been deemed trivial didn't feel that way, and that was when the disappearance services cropped up. If a person disappeared and could not be found, most alien groups kept an outstanding warrant, but stopped searching.

The Disty never did.

And since much of the Third Dynasty's business was conducted in Disty territory, its disappearance service, Privacy Unlimited, had to be one of the best in the galaxy.

Something in my face must have given my knowledge away, because she said, "Now do you understand my problem?"

"Frankly, no," I said. "You're the daughter of the big kahuna. Go to Privacy Unlimited and have them help you. It's usually not too hard to retrace steps."

She shook her head. "My mother didn't go to Privacy Unlimited. She used another service."

"You're sure?"

"Yes." She brushed a hand alongside her head, to move the long hair. "It's my father she's running from."

A domestic situation. I never get involved in those. Too messy and too complicated. Never a clear line. "Then she didn't need a service at all. She probably took a shuttle here, then a transport for parts unknown."

Anetka Sobol crossed her arms. "You don't seem to understand, Mr. Flint. My father could have found her with his own service if she had done something like that. It's simple enough. My detectives should have been able to find her. They can't."

"Let me see if I can understand this," I said. "Are you looking for her or is your father?"

"I am."

"As a front for him?"

Color flooded her face. "No."

"Then why?"

"I want to meet her."

I snorted. "You're going to a lot of expense for a 'hello, how are you.' Aren't you afraid Daddy will find out?"

"I have my own money."

"Really? Money Daddy doesn't know about? Money Daddy doesn't monitor?"

She straightened. "He doesn't monitor me."

I nodded. "That's why the mesh gloves. Fashion statement?"

She glanced at her enhancements. "I got them. They have nothing to do with my father."

My smile was small. "Your father has incredible resources. You don't think he'd do something as simple as hack into your enhancement files. Believe me, one of those pretty baubles is being used to track you, and if my security weren't as good as it is, another would have been monitoring this conversation."

She put her left hand over her right as if covering the enhancements would make me forget them. All it did was remind me that this time, she didn't react when my security shut down her links. This was one smart girl, and one I didn't entirely understand.

"Go home," I said. "Deal with Daddy. If you want family ties, get married, have children, hire someone to play your mother. If you need genetic information or disease history, see your family doctors. I suspect they'll have all the records you need and probably some you don't. If you want Daddy to leave you alone, I'd ask him first before I go to any more expense. He might just do what you want. And if you're trying to make him angry, I'll bet you've gone far enough. You'll probably be hearing from him very soon."

Her eyes narrowed. "You're so sure of yourself, Mr. Flint."

"It's about the only thing I am sure of," I said, and waited for her to leave.

She didn't. She stared at me for a long moment, and in her eyes, I saw a coldness, a hardness I hadn't expected. It was as if she were evaluating me and finding me lacking.

I let her stare. I didn't care what she thought one way or another. I did wish she would get to the point so that I could kick her out of my office.

Finally she sighed and pursed her lips as if she had eaten something sour. She looked around, probably searching for some place to sit down. She didn't find one. I don't like my clients to sit. I don't want them to be comfortable in my presence.

"All right," she said, and her voice was somehow different. Stronger, a little more powerful. I knew the timidity had been an act. "I came to you because you seem to be the only one who can do this job."

My smile was crooked and insincere. "Flattery."

"Truth," she said.

I shook my head. "There are dozens of people who do this job, and most are cheaper." I let my smile grow colder. "They also have chairs in their offices."

"They value their clients," she said.

"Probably at the expense of the people they're searching out."

"Ethics," she said. "That's why I've come here. You're the only one in your profession who seems to have any."

"You have need of ethics?" Somehow I had trouble believing the woman with that powerful voice had need of anyone with ethics. "Or is this simply another attempt at manipulation?"

To my surprise, she smiled. The expression was stunning. It brought life to her eyes, and somehow seemed to make her even taller than she had been a moment before.

"Manipulation got me to you," she said. "Your Mr. Gonnot seems to have a soft spot for people who are missing family."

"Everyone who's missing is a member of a family," I said, but more to the absent Gonnot than to her. I could see how he could be manipulated, and that made it more important than ever to stop him from sending customers my way.

She shrugged at my comment, then she sat on the edge of my desk. I'd never had anyone do that, not in all my years in the business. "I do have need of ethics," she said. "If you breathe a single word of what I'm going to tell you…"

She didn't finish the sentence, on purpose of course, probably figuring that whatever I could imagine would be worse than what she could come up with.

I sighed. This girl—this woman—liked games.

"If you want the sanctity of a confessional," I said, "see a priest. If you want a profession that requires its practitioners to practice confidentiality as a matter of course, see a psychiatrist. I'll keep confidential whatever I deem worthy of confidentiality."

She folded her slender hands on her lap. "You enjoy judging your clients, don't you?"

I stared at her—up at her—which actually put me at a disadvantage. She was good at intimidation skills, even better than she had been as an actress. It made me uncomfortable, but somehow it seemed more logical for the daughter of the man who ran the Third Dynasty.

"I have to," I said. "A lot of lives depend on my judgments."

She shook her head slightly. It was as if my earlier answer stymied her, prevented her from continuing. She had to learn that we would do this on my terms or we wouldn't do it at all.

I waited. I could wait all day if I had to. Most people didn't have that kind of patience no matter what sort of will they had.

She clearly didn't. After a few moments, she brushed her pants, adjusted the flap on one of the pockets, and sighed again. She must have needed me badly.

Finally, she closed her eyes, as if summoning strength. When she opened them, she was looking at me directly. "I am a clone, Mr. Flint."

Whatever I had thought she was going to say, it wasn't that. I worked very hard at keeping the surprise off my face.

"And my father is dying." She paused, as if she were testing me.

I knew the answer, and the problem. When her father died, she couldn't inherit. Clones were barred from familial inheritance by interstellar law. The law had been adapted universally after several cases where clones created by a non-family member and raised far from the original (wealthy) family inherited vast estates. The basis of the inheritance was a shared biology that anyone could create. Rather than letting large fortunes get leached off to whoever was smart enough to steal a hair from a hairbrush and use it to create a copy of a human being, legislators finally decided to create the law. The courts upheld it. It was rigid.

"Your father could change his will," I said, knowing that she had probably broached this with him already.

"It's too late," she said. "He's been ill for a while. The change could easily be disputed in court."

"So you're not an only child?" I had to work to keep from asking if she were an only copy.

"I am the only clone," she said. "My father had me made, and he raised me himself. I am, for all intents and purposes, his daughter."

"Then he should have changed his will long ago."

She waved a hand, as if the very idea were a silly one. And it probably was. A clone had to come from somewhere. So either she was the copy of a real child or a copy of the woman she wanted me to find. Perhaps the will was unchanged because the original person was still out there.

"My mother vanished with the real heir," she said.

I waited.

"My father always expected to find them. My sister is the one who inherits."

I hated clone terminology. "Sister" was such an inaccurate term, even though clones saw themselves as twins. They weren't. They weren't raised that way or thought of that way. The Original stood to inherit. The clone before me did not.

"So you, out of the goodness of your heart, are searching for your missing family." I laid the sarcasm on thick. I've handled similar cases before. Where money was involved, people were rarely altruistic.

"No," she said, and her bluntness surprised me. "My father owns 51% of the Third Dynasty. When he dies, it goes into the corporation itself, and can be bought by other shareholders. I am not a shareholder, but I have been raised from birth to run the Dynasty. The idea was that I would share my knowledge with my sister, and that we would run the business together."

This made more sense.

"So I need to find her, Mr. Flint, before the shares go back into the corporation. I need to find her so that I can live the kind of life I was raised to live."

I hated cases like this. She was right. I did judge my clients. And if I found them the least bit suspicious, I didn't take on the case. If I believed that what they would do would jeopardize the Disappeared, I wouldn't take the case either. But if the reason for the disappearance was gone, or if the reason for finding the missing person benefited or did not harm the Disappeared, then I would take the case.

I saw benefit here, in the inheritance, and in the fact that the reason for the disappearance was dying.

"Your father willed his entire fortune to his missing child?"
She nodded.

"Then why isn't he searching for her?"

"He figured she would come back when she heard of his death."

Possible, depending on where she had disappeared to, but not entirely probable. The girl might not even know who she was.

"If I find your mother," I said, "then will your father try to harm her?"

"No," she said. "He couldn't if he wanted to. He's too sick. I can forward the medical records to you."

One more thing to check. And check I would. I guess I was taking this case, no matter how messily she started it. I was intrigued, just enough.

"Your father doesn't have to be healthy enough to act on his own," I said. "With his money, he could hire someone."

"I suppose," she said. "But I control almost all of his business dealings right now. The request would have to go through me."

I still didn't like it, but superficially, it sounded fine. I would, of course, check it out. "Where's your clone mark?"

She frowned at me. It was a rude question, but one I needed the answer to before I started.

She pulled her hair back, revealing a small number eight at the spot where her skull met her neck. The fine hairs had grown away from it, and the damage to the skin had been done at the cellular level. If she tried to have the eight removed, it would grow back.

"What happened to the other seven?" I asked.

She let her hair fall. "Failed."

Failed clones were unusual. Anything unusual in a case like this was suspect.

"My mother," she said, as if she could hear my thoughts, "was pregnant when she disappeared. I was cloned from sloughed cells found in the amnio."

"Hers or the baby's?"

"The baby's. They tested. But they used a lot of cells to find one that worked. It took a while before they got me."

Sounded plausible, but I was no expert. More information to check.

"Your father must have wanted you badly."

She nodded.

"Seems strange that he didn't alter his will for you."

Her shoulders slumped. "He was afraid any changes he made wouldn't have been lawyer-proof. He was convinced I'd lose everything because of lawsuits if he did that."

"So he arranged for you to lose everything on his own."

She shook her head. "He wanted the family together. He wanted me to work with my sister to—"

"So he said."

"So he says." She ran a hand through her hair. "I think he hopes that my sister will cede the company to me. For a percentage, of course."

There it was. The only loophole in the law. A clone could receive an inheritance if it came directly from the person whose genetic material the clone shared, provided that the Original couldn't die under suspicious circumstances. Of course, a living person could, in Anetka's words, "cede" that ownership as well, although it was a bit more difficult.

"You're looking for her for money," I said in my last ditch effort to get out of the case.

"You won't believe love," she said.

She was right. I wouldn't have.

"Besides," she said. "I have my own money. More than enough to keep me comfortable for the rest of my life. Whatever else you may think of my father, he has provided that. I'm searching for her for the corporation. I want to keep it in the family. I want to work it like I was trained. And this seems to be the only way."

It wasn't a very pretty reason, and I'd learned over the years, it was usually the ugly reasons that were the truth. Not, of course, that I could go by gut. I wouldn't.

"My retainer is two million credits," I said. "If you're lucky, that's all this investigation will cost you. I have a contract that I'll send to you or your personal representative, but let me give you the short version verbally."

She nodded.

I continued, reciting, as I always did, the essential terms so that no client could ever say I'd lied to her. "I have the right to terminate at any time for any reason. You may not terminate until the Disappeared is found, or I have concluded that the Disappeared is gone for good. You are legally liable for any lawsuits that arise from any crimes committed by third parties as a result of this investigation. I am not. You will pay me my rate plus expenses whenever I bill you. If your money stops, the investigation stops, but if I find you've been withholding funds to prevent me from digging farther, I am entitled to a minimum of ten million credits. I will begin my investigation by investigating you. Should I decide you are unworthy as a client before I begin searching for the Disappeared, I will refund half of your initial retainer. There's more but those are the salient points. Is all of that clear?"

"Perfectly."

"I'll begin as soon as I get the retainer."

"Give me your numbers and I'll have the money placed in your account immediately."

I handed her my single printed card with my escrow account embedded into it. The account was a front for several other accounts, but she didn't need to know that. Even my money went through channels. Someone who is good at finding the Disappeared is also good at making other things disappear.

"Should you need to reach me in an emergency," I said, "place 673 credits into this account."

"Strange number," she said.

I nodded. The number varied from client to client, a random pattern. Sometimes, past clients sent me their old amounts as a way to contact me about something new. I kept the system clear.

"I'll respond to the depositing computer from wherever I am, as soon as I can. This is not something you should do frivolously nor is it something to be done to check up on me. It's only for an emergency. If you want to track the progress of the investigation, you can wait for my weekly updates."

"And if I have questions?"

"Save them for later."

"What if I think I can help?"

"Leave me mail." I stood. She was watching me, that hard edge in her eyes again. "I've got work to do now. I'll contact you when I'm ready to begin my search."

"How long will this investigation of me take?"

"I have no idea," I said. "It depends on how much you're hiding."

4

CLIENTS NEVER TELL the truth. No matter how much I instruct them to, they never do. It seems to be human nature to lie about something, even it's something small. I had a hunch, given Anetka Sobol's background, she had lied about a lot. The catch was to find out how much of what she had lied about was relevant to the job she had hired me for. Finding out required research.

I do a lot of my research through public accounts, using fake i.d. It is precautionary, particularly in the beginning, because so many cases don't pan out. If a Disappeared still has a Tracker after her, repeated searches from me will be flagged. Searches from public accounts—especially different public accounts—will not. Often the Disappeared are already famous or become famous when they vanish, and are often the subject of anything from vidspec to school reports.

My favorite search site is a bar not too far from my office. I love the place because it serves some of the best food in Armstrong, in some of the largest quantities. The large quantities are required, given the place's name. The Brownie Bar serves the only marijuana in the area, baked into specially marked goods, particularly the aforementioned brownies. Imbibers get the munchies, and proceed to spend hundreds of credits on food. The place turns quite a profit, and it's also comfortable; marijuana users seem to like their creature comforts more than most other recreational drug types.

Recreational drugs are legal on the Moon, as are most things. The first settlers came in search of something they called "freedom from oppression" which usually meant freedom to pursue an alternative lifestyle. Some of those lifestyles have since become illegal or simply died out, but others remain. The only illegal drugs these days, at least in Armstrong, are those that interfere with the free flow of air. Everything from nicotine to opium is legal—as long as its user doesn't smoke it.

The Brownie Bar caters to the casual user as well as the hard-core and, unlike some drug bars, doesn't mind the non-user customer. The interior is large, with several sections. One section, the party wing, favors the bigger groups, the ones who usually arrive in numbers larger than ten, spend hours eating and giggling, and often get quite obnoxiously wacky. In the main section, soft booths with tables shield clients from each other. Usually the people sitting there are couples or groups of four. If one group gets particularly loud, a curtain drops over the open section of the booth, and their riotous laughter fades into nearly nothing.

My section caters to the hard-core, who sometimes stop for a quick fix in the middle of the business day, or who like a brownie before dinner to calm the stress of a hectic afternoon. Many of these people have only one, and continue work while they're sitting at their solitary tables. It's quiet as a church in this section, and many of the patrons are plugged into the free client ports that allow them access to the Net.

The access ports are free, but the information is not. Particular servers charge by the hour in the public areas, but have the benefit of allowing me to troll using the server or the bar's identicodes. I like that; it usually makes my preliminary searches impossible to trace.

That afternoon, I took my usual table in the very back. It's small, made of high grade plastic designed to look like wood—and it fools most people. It never fooled me, partly because I knew the Brownie Bar couldn't afford to import, and partly because I knew they'd never risk something that valuable on a restaurant designed for stoners. I sat cross-legged on the thick pillow on the floor, ordered some turkey stew—made here with real meat— and plugged in.

The screen was tabletop, and had a keyboard so that the user could have complete privacy. I'd heard other patrons complain that using the Brownie Bar's system required them to read, but it was one of the features I liked.

I started with Anetka, and decided to work my way backwards through the Sobol family. I found her quickly enough; her life was well covered by the tabs, which made no mention of her clone status. She was twenty-seven, ten to twelve years older than she looked. She'd apparently had those youthful looks placed in stasis surgically. She'd look girlish until she died.

Another good fact to know. If there was an original, she might not look like Anetka. Not any more.

Anetka had been working in her father's corporation since she was twelve. Her IQ was off the charts—surgically enhanced as well, at least according to most of the vidspec programs—and she breezed through Harvard and then Cambridge. She did postdoc work at the Interstellar Business School in Islamabad, and was out of school by the time she was twenty-five. For the last two years, she'd been on the corporate fast-track, starting in lower management and working her way to the top of the corporate ladder.

She was, according to the latest feeds, her father's main assistant.

So I had already found Possible Lie Number One: She wasn't here for herself. She was, as I had suspected, a front for her father. Not to find the wife, but to find the real heir.

I wasn't sure how I'd feel if that were true. I needed to find out if, indeed, the Original was the one who'd inherit. If she wasn't, I wouldn't take the case. There'd be no point.

But I wasn't ready to make judgments yet. I had a long way to go. I looked up Anetka's father, and discovered that Carson Sobol had never remarried, although he'd been seen with a bevy of beautiful women over the years. All were close to his age. He never dated women younger than he was. Most had their own fortunes, and many their own companies. He spent several years as the companion to an acclaimed Broadway actress, even funding some of her more famous plays. That relationship, like the others, had ended amicably.

Which led to Possible Lie Number Two: a man who terrorized his wife so badly that she had to run away from him also terrorized his later girlfriends. And while a man could keep something like that quiet for a few years, eventually the pattern would become evident. Eventually one of the women would talk.

There was no evidence of terrorizing in the stuff I found. Perhaps the incidences weren't reported. Or perhaps there was nothing to report. I would vote for the latter. It seemed, from the vidspec I'd read, everyone knew that the wife had left him because of his cruelty. My experience with vidspec reporters made me confident that they'd be on the lookout for more proof of Carson Sobol's nasty character. And if they found it, they'd report it.

No one had.

I didn't know if that meant Sobol had learned his lesson when the wife ran off, or perhaps Sobol had learned that mistreatment of women was bad for business. I couldn't believe that a man could terrify everyone into silence. If that were his methodology, there would be a few leaks that were quickly hushed up, and one or two dead bodies floating around, bodies belonging to folks who hadn't listened. Also, there would be rumors, and there were none.

Granted, I was making assumptions on a very small amount of information. Most of the reports I found about

Sobol weren't about his family or his love life, but about the Third Dynasty as it expanded in that period to new worlds, places that human businesses had never been before.

The Third Dynasty had been the first to do business with the Fuetrers, the HDs, and the chichers. It opened plants on Korsve, then closed them when it realized that the Wygnin, the dominant life forms on Korsve, did not— and apparently could not—understand the way that humans did business.

I shuddered at the mention of Korsve. If a client approached me because a family member had been taken by the Wygnin, I refused the case. The Wygnin took individuals to pay off debt, and then those individuals became part of a particular Wygnin family. For particularly heinous crimes, the Wygnin took firstborns, but usually, the Wygnin just took babies—from any place in the family structure—at the time of birth, and then raised them. Occasionally they'd take an older child or an adult. Sometimes they'd take an entire group of adults from offending businesses. The adults were subject to mind control, and personality destruction as the Wygnin tried to remake them to fit into Wygnin life.

All of that left me with no good options. Children raised by the Wygnin considered themselves Wygnin and couldn't adapt to human cultures. Adults who were taken by the Wygnin were so broken that they were almost unrecognizable. Humans raised by the Wygnin did not want to return. Adults who were broken always wanted to return, and when they did, they signed a death warrant for their entire family—or worse, doomed an entire new generation to kidnap by the Wygnin.

But Wygnin custom didn't seem relevant here. Despite the plant closings, the Third Dynasty had managed to avoid paying a traditional Wygnin price. Or perhaps someone had paid, down the line, and that information was classified.

There were other possibles in the files. The Third Dynasty seemed to have touched every difficult alien race in the galaxy. The corporation had an entire division set aside for dealing with new cultures. Not that the division was infallible. Sometimes there were unavoidable errors.

Sylvy Sobol's disappearance had been one of those. It had caused all sorts of problems for both Sobol and the Third Dynasty. The vidspecs, tabs, and other media had had a field day when she had disappeared. The news led to problems with some of the alien races, particularly the Altaden. The Altaden valued non-violence above all else, and the accusations of domestic violence at the top levels of the Third Dynasty nearly cost the corporation its Altade holdings.

The thing was, no one expected the disappearance— or the marriage, for that matter. Sylvy Sobol had been a European socialite, better known for her charitable works and her incredible beauty than her interest in business. She belonged to an old family with ties to several still existing monarchies. It was thought that her marriage would be to someone else from the accepted circle.

It had caused quite a scandal when she had chosen Carson Sobol, not only because of his mixed background and uncertain lineage, but also because some of his business practices had taken large fortunes from the countries she was tied to and spent them in space instead.

He was controversial; the marriage was controversial; and it looked like, from the vids I watched, that the two of them had been deeply in love.

I felt a hand on my shoulder. A waitress stood behind me, holding a large ceramic bowl filled with turkey stew. She smiled at me.

"Didn't want to set it on your work."

"It's fine," I said, indicating an empty spot near the screen. She set my utensils down, and then the bowl. The stew smelled rich and fine, black beans and yogurt adding to the aroma. My stomach growled.

The waitress tapped one of the moving images. "I remember that," she said. "I was living in Vienna. The Viennese thought that marriage was an abomination."

I looked up. She was older than I was, without the funds to prevent the natural aging process. Laugh lines crinkled around her eyes, and her lips—unpainted and untouched—were a faint rose. She smiled.

"Guess it turned out that way, huh? The wife running off like that? Leaving that message?"

"Message?" I asked. I hadn't gotten that far.

"I don't remember exactly what it was. Something like 'The long arm of the Third Dynasty is impossible to fight. I am going where you can't find me. Maybe then I'll have the chance to live out my entire life.' I guess he nearly beat her to death." The waitress laughed, a little embarrassed.

177

"In those days I had nothing better to do than study the lives of more interesting people."

"And now?" I asked.

She shrugged. "I figured out that everybody's interesting. I mean, you've got to try. You've got to live. And if you do, you've done something fascinating."

I nodded. People like her were one of the reasons I liked this place.

"You want something to drink?" she asked.

"Bottled water."

"Got it," she said as she left.

By the time she brought my bottled water, I had indeed found the note. It had been sent to all the broadcast media, along with a grainy video, taken from a hidden camera, of one of the most brutal domestic beatings I'd ever seen. The images were sometimes blurred and indistinct, but the actions were clear. The man had beat the woman senseless.

There was no mention of the pregnancy in any of this. There was, however, notification of Anetka's birth six months before her mother had disappeared.

Which led me to Possible Lie Number Three. Anetka had said her mother traveled pregnant. Perhaps she hadn't. Or, more chillingly, someone had altered the record either before or after the clones were brought to term. There had to be an explanation of Anetka in the media or she wouldn't be accepted. If that explanation had been planted before, something else was going on. If it were planted afterwards, Sobol's spokespeople could have simply said that reporters had overlooked her in their rush to other stories.

I checked the other media reports and found the same story. It was time to go beneath those stories and see what else I could find. Then I would confront Anetka about the lies before I began the search for her mother.

5

I CONTACTED HER and we met, not at my office, but at her hotel. She was staying in Armstrong's newest district, an addition onto the dome that caused a terrible controversy before it was built. Folks in my section believe the reason for the thinner air is that the new addition has stretched resources. I know they aren't right—with the addition came more air and all the other regulation equipment—but it was one of those arguments that made an emotional kind of sense.

I thought of those arguments, though, as I walked among the new buildings, made from a beige material not even conceived of thirty years before, a material that's supposed to be attractive (it isn't) and more resistant to decay that permaplastic. This entire section of Armstrong smelled new, from the recycled air to the buildings rising around me. They were four stories high and had large windows on the dome side, obviously built with a view in mind.

This part of the dome is self-cleaning and see-through. Dust does not slowly creep up the sides as it does in the other parts of Armstrong. The view is barren and stark, just like the rest of the Moon, but there's a beauty in the starkness that I don't see anywhere else in the universe.

The hotel was another large four story building. Most of its windows were glazed dark, so no one could see in, but the patrons could see out. It was part of a chain whose parent company was, I had learned the day before, the Third Dynasty. Anetka was doing very little to hide her search from her father.

Inside, the lobby was wide, and had an old-fashioned feel. The walls changed images slowly, showing the famous sites from various parts of the galaxy where the hotels were located. I had read before the hotel opened that the constantly changing scenery took eight weeks to repeat an image. I wondered what it was like working in a place where the view shifted constantly, and then decided I didn't want to know.

The lobby furniture was soft and a comforting shade of dove gray. Piano music, equally soft and equally comforting, was piped in from somewhere. Patrons sat in small groups as if they were posing for a brochure. I went up to the main desk and asked for Anetka. The concierge led me to a private conference room down the main hallway.

I expected the room to be monitored. That didn't bother me. At this point, I still had nothing to hide. Anetka did, but this was her company's hotel. She could get the records, shut off the monitors, or have them destroyed. It would all be her choice.

To my surprise, she was waiting for me. She was wearing another dress, a blue diaphanous thing that looked so fragile I wondered how she managed to move from place to place. Her hair was up and pinned, with diamonds glinting from the soft folds. She also had diamonds glued to the ridge beneath her eyebrows, and trailing down her cheeks. The net effect was to accent her strength. Her broad shoulders held the gown as if it were air, and the folds parted to reveal the muscles on her arms and legs. She was like the diamonds she wore; pretty and glittering, but able to cut through all the objects in the room.

"Have you found anything?" she asked without preamble.

I shut the door and helped myself to the carafe of water on the bar against the nearest wall. There was a table in the center of the room—made, it seemed—of real wood, with matching chairs on the side. There was also a workstation, and a one-way mirror with a view of the lobby.

I leaned against the bar, holding my water glass. It was thick and heavy, sturdy like most things on the Moon. "Your father's will has been posted among the Legal Notices on all the nets for the last three years."

She nodded. "It's common for CEOs to do that to allay stockholder fears."

"It's common for CEOs to authorize the release after they've died. Not before."

Her smile was small, almost patronizing. "Smaller corporations, yes. But it's becoming a requirement for major shareholders in megacorps to do this even if they are not dead. Investigate further, Mr. Flint, and you'll see that all of the Third Dynasty's major shareholders have posted their wills."

I had already checked the other shareholders' wills, and found that Anetka was right. I also looked for evidence that Carson Sobol was dead, and found none.

She took my silence to be disbelief. "It's the same with the other megacorps. Personal dealings are no longer private in the galactic business world."

I had known that the changes were taking place. I had known, for example, that middle managers signed loyalty oaths to corporations, sometimes requiring them to forsake family if the corporation had called for it. This, one pundit had said, was the hidden cost of doing business with alien races. You had to be willing to abandon all you knew in the advent of a serious mistake. The upshot of the change was becoming obvious. People to whom family was important were staying away from positions of power in the megacorps.

I said, "You're not going to great lengths to hide this search from your father."

She placed a hand on the wooden chair. She was not wearing gloves, and mingled among the enhancements were more diamonds. "You seem obsessed with my father."

"Your mother disappeared because of him. I'm not going to find her only to have him kill her."

"He wouldn't."

"Says you."

"This is your hesitation?"

"Actually, no," I said. "My hesitation is that, according to all public records, you were born six months before your mother disappeared."

I didn't tell her that I knew all the databases had been tampered with, including the ones about her mother's disappearance. I couldn't tell if the information had been altered to show that the disappearance came later or that the child had been born earlier. The tampering was so old that the original material was lost forever.

"My father wanted me to look like a legitimate child."

"You are a clone. He knew cloning laws."

"But no one else had to know."

"Not even with his will posted?"

"I told you. It's only been posted for the last three years."

"Is that why you're not mentioned?"

She raised her chin. "I received my inheritance before—already," she said. I found the correction interesting. "The agreement between us about my sister is both confidential and binding."

"'All of my worldly possessions shall go to my eldest child,'" I quoted. "That child isn't even listed by name."

"No," she said.

"And he isn't going to change the will for you?"

"The Disty won't do business with clones."

"I didn't know you had business with the Disty," I said.

She shrugged. "The Disty, the Emin, the Revs. You name them, we have business with them. And we have to be careful of some customs."

"Won't the stockholders be suspicious when you don't inherit?"

Her mouth formed a thin line. "That's why I'm hiring you," she said. "You need to find my sister."

I nodded. Then, for the first time in the meeting, I sat down. The chair was softer than I had expected it would be. I put my feet on the nearest chair. She glanced at them as if they were a lower life form.

"In order to search for people," I said, "I need to know who they're running from. If they're running from the Disty, for example, I'll avoid the Martian colonies, because they're overrun with Disty. No one would hide there. It would be impossible. If they were running from the Revs, I would start looking at plastic surgeons and doctors who specialize in genetic alteration because anyone who looks significantly different from the person the Revs have targeted is considered, by the Revs, to be a different being entirely."

She started to say something, but I held up my hand to silence her.

"Human spouses abuse each other," I said. "It seems to be part of the human experience. These days, the abused spouse moves out, and sometimes leaves the city, sometimes the planet, but more often than not stays in the same area. It's unusual to run, to go through a complete identity change, and to start a new life, especially in your parents' income bracket. So tell me, why did your mother really leave?"

Nothing changed in Anetka's expression. It remained so immobile that I knew she was struggling for control.

The hardness that had been so prevalent the day before was gone, banished, it seemed, so that I wouldn't see anything amiss.

"My father has a lot of money," she said.

"So do other people. Their spouses don't disappear."

"He also controls a powerful megacorp with fingers all over the developing worlds. He has access to more information than anyone. He vowed to never let my mother out of his sight. My father believed that marriage vows were sacred, and no matter how much the parties wanted out, they were obligated by their promises to each other and to God to remain." Anetka's tone was flat too. "If she had just moved out, he would have forced her to move back in. If she had moved to the Moon, he would have come after her. If she had moved to some of the planets in the next solar system, he would have come for her. So she had no choice."

"According to your father."

"According to anyone who knew her." Anetka's voice was soft. "You saw the vids."

I nodded.

"That was mild, I guess, for what he did to her."

I leaned back in the chair, lifting the front two legs off the ground. "So how come he didn't treat his other women that way?"

Something passed through her eyes so quickly that I wasn't able to see what the expression was. Suspicion? Fear? I couldn't tell.

"My father never allowed himself to get close to anyone else."

"Not even his Broadway actress?"

She frowned, then said, "Oh, Linda? No. Not even her. They were using each other to throw off the media. She had a more significant relationship with one of the major critics, and she didn't want that to get out."

"What about you?" I asked that last softly. "If he hurt your mother, why didn't he hurt you?"

She put her other hand on the chair as if she were steadying herself. "Who says he didn't?"

And in that flatness of tone, I heard all the complaints I'd ever heard from clones. She had legal protection, of course. She was fully human. But she didn't have familial protection. She wasn't part of any real group. She didn't have defenders, except those she hired herself.

But I didn't believe it, not entirely. She was still lying to me. She was still keeping me slightly off balance. Something was missing, but I couldn't find it. I'd done all the digging I could reasonably do. I had no direction to go except after the missing wife—if I chose to continue working on this case. This was the last point at which I could comfortably extricate myself from the entire mess.

"You're not telling me everything," I said.

Again, the movement with the eyes. So subtle. So quick. I wondered if she had learned to cover up her emotions from her father.

"My father won't harm her," she said. "If you want, I'll even sign a waiver guaranteeing that."

It seemed the perfect solution to a superficial problem. I had a hunch there were other problems lurking below.

"I'll have one sent to you," I said.

"Are you still taking the case?"

"Are you still lying to me?"

She paused, the dress billowing around her in the static-charged air. "I need you to find my sister," she said.

And that much, we both knew to be true.

6

MY WORK IS NINE-TENTHS research and one-tenth excitement. Most of the research comes in the beginning, and it's dry to most people, although I still find the research fascinating. It's also idiosyncratic and part of the secret behind my reputation. I usually don't describe how I do the research—and I never explain it to clients. I usually summarize it, like this:

It took me four months to do the preliminary research on Sylvy Sobol. I started from the premise that she was pregnant with a single girl child. A pregnant woman did one of three things: she carried the baby to term, she miscarried, or she aborted. After dealing with hospital records for what seemed like weeks, I determined that she carried the baby to term. Or at least, she hadn't gotten rid of it before she disappeared.

A pregnant woman had fewer relocation options than a non-pregnant one. She couldn't travel as far or on many forms of transport because it might harm the fetus. Several planets, hospitable to humans after they'd acclimatized, were not places someone in the middle of pregnancy was allowed to go. The pregnancy actually made my job easier, and I was glad for it.

Whoever had hidden her was good, but no disappearance service was perfect. They all had cracks in their systems, some revealing themselves in certain types of disappearance, others in all cases past a certain layer of complexity. I knew those flaws as well as I knew the scars and blemishes on my own hands. And I exploited them with ease.

At the end of four months, I had five leads on the former Mrs. Sobol. At the end of five months, I had eliminated two of those leads. At the end of six months, I had a pretty good idea which of the remaining three leads was the woman I was looking for.

I got in my ship, and headed for Mars.

7

IN THE HUNDRED YEARS since the Disty first entered this solar system, they have taken over Mars. The human-run mineral operations and the ship bases are still there, but the colonies are all Disty run, and some are Disty built.

The Emmeline has clearance on most planets where humans make their homes. Mars is no difference. I docked at the Dunes, above the Arctic Circle, and wished I were going elsewhere. It was the Martian winter, and here, in the largest field of sand dunes in the solar system, that meant several months of unrelenting dark.

I had never understood how the locals put up with this. But I hadn't understood a lot of things. The domes here, mostly of human construction, had an artificial lighting system built in, but the Disty hated the approximation of a twenty-four hour day. Since the Disty had taken over the northern most colonies, darkness outside and artificial lights inside were the hallmarks of winter.

The Disty made other alterations as well. The Disty were small creatures with large heads, large eyes, and narrow bodies. They hated the feeling of wide open spaces, and so in many parts of the Sahara Dome, as Terrans called this place, false ceilings had been built in, and corridors had been compressed. Buildings were added into the wider spaces, getting rid of many passageways and making the entire place seem like a rat's warren. Most adult humans had to crouch to walk comfortably through the city streets and some, in disgust, had bought small carts so that they could ride. The result was a congestion that I found claustrophobic at the best of times. I hated crouching when I walked, and I hated the stink of so many beings in such a confined space.

Many Terran buildings rose higher than the ceiling level of the street, but to discourage that wide-open spaces feel, the Disty built more structures, many of them so close together that there was barely enough room for a human to stick his arm between them. Doors lined the crowded streets, and the only identifying marks on most places were carved into the frame along the door's side. The carvings were difficult to see in the weird lighting, even if there weren't the usual crowds struggling to get through the streets to God knew where.

My candidate lived in a building owned by the Disty. It took me two passes to find the building's number, and another to realize that I had found the right place. A small sign, in English, advertised accommodations fit for humans, and my back and I hoped that the sign was right.

It was. The entire building had been designed with humans in mind. The Disty had proven themselves to be able interstellar traders, and quite willing to adapt to local customs when it suited them. It showed in the interior design of this place. Once I stepped through the door, I was able to stand upright, although the top of my head did brush the ceiling. To my left, a sign pointed toward the main office, another pointed to some cramped stairs, and a third pointed to the recreation area.

I glanced at the main office before I explored any farther. The office was up front, and had the same human-sized ceilings. In order to cope, the Disty running the place sat on its desk, its long feet pressed together in concentration. I passed it, and went to the recreation area. I would look for the woman here before I went door to door upstairs.

The recreation area was about half the size of a human-made room for the same purpose. Still, the Disty managed to cram a lot of stuff in here, and the closeness of everything—while comfortable for the Disty—made it uncomfortable for any human. All five humans in the room were huddled near the bar on the far end. It was the only place with a walking path large enough to allow a full-grown man through.

To get there, I had to go past the ping-pong table, and a small section set aside for Go players. Several Disty were playing Go—they felt it was the best thing they had discovered on the planet Earth, with ping-pong a close second—sitting on the tables so that their heads were as near the ceiling as they could get. Two more Disty were standing on the table, playing ping-pong. None of them paid me any attention at all.

I wound my way through the tight space between the Go players and the ping-pong table, ducking once to avoid being whapped in the head with an out-of-control ping-pong ball. I noted three other Disty watching the games with rapt interest. The humans, on the other hand, had their backs to the rest of the room. They were sitting on the tilting bar stools, drinking, and not looking too happy about anything.

A woman who could have been anywhere from thirty to seventy-five sat at one end of the bar. Her black hair fell to the middle of her back, and she wore make-up, an affectation that the Disty seemed to like. She was slender—anyone who wanted to live comfortably here had to be—and she wore a silver beaded dress that accented that slimness. Her legs were smooth, and did not bear any marks from mining or other harsh work.

"Susan Wilcox?" I asked as I put my hand on her shoulder and showed her my license.

I felt the tension run through her body, followed by several shivers, but her face gave no sign that anything was wrong.

"Want to go talk?"

She smiled at me, a smooth professional smile that made me feel a little more comfortable. "Sure."

She stood, took my hand as if we'd been friends a long time, and led me onto a little patio someone had cobbled together in a tiny space behind the recreation area. I didn't see the point of the thing until I looked up. This was one of the few places in Sahara where the dome was visible, and through its clear surface, you could see the sky. She pulled over a chair, and I grabbed one as well.

"How did you find me?" she asked.

"I'm not sure I did." I held out my hand. In it was one of my palmtop. "I want to do a DNA check."

She raised her chin slightly. "That's not legal."

"I could get a court order."

She looked at me. A court order would ruin any protection she had, no matter who—or what—she was running from.

"I'm not going to see who you are. I want to see if you're who I'm looking for. I have comparison DNA."

"You're lying," she said softly.

"Maybe," I said. "If I am, you're in trouble either way."

She knew I was right. She could either take her chances with me, or face the court order where she had no chance at all.

She extended her hand. I ran the edge of the computer along her palm, removing skin cells. The comparison program ran, and as I turned the palmtop face-up, I saw that there was no match. The only thing this woman shared in common with the former Mrs. Sobol was that they were both females of a similar age, and that they had both disappeared twenty-nine years ago while pregnant. Almost everything else was different.

I used my wrist-top for a double-check, and then I sighed. She was watching me closely, her dark eyes reflecting the light from inside.

I smiled at her. "You're in the clear," I said. "But if it was this easy for me to find you, chances are that it'll be as easy for someone else. You might want to move on."

She shook her head once, as if the very idea were repugnant.

"Your child might appreciate it," I said.

She looked at me as if I had struck her. "She's not who—"

"No," I said. "She's safe. From me at least. And maybe from whoever's after you. But you've survived out here nearly thirty years. You know the value of caution."

She swallowed, hard. "You know a lot about me."

"Not really." I stood. "I only know what you have in common with the woman I'm looking for." I slipped the palmtop into my pocket and bowed slightly. "I appreciate your time."

Then I went back inside, slipped through the recreation area, walked past two more Disty in the foyer, and headed into the narrow passageway they called a street. There I shuddered. I hated the Disty. I'd worked so many cases in which people ran to avoid being caught by the Disty that I'd become averse to them myself.

At least, that was my explanation for my shudder. But I knew that it wasn't a real explanation. I had put a woman's life in jeopardy, and we both knew it. I hoped no one had been paying attention. But I was probably wrong. The only solace I had was that since she was hiding amongst the Disty, she probably wasn't being sought by one of them. If she had been pursued by a Disty, my actions probably would have signed her death warrant.

I spent a night in a cramped hotel room since the Disty didn't allow take-offs within thirty-six hours of landing. And then I got the hell away from Sahara Dome—and Mars.

8

My second possibility was in New Orleans, which made my task a lot easier. I had former clients there who felt they owed me, some of whom were in related businesses. I had one of those clients break into the Disappeared's apartment, remove a strand of hair, and give it to another former client. A third brought me the strand in my room in the International Space Station. Because the strand proved not to be a match, and because I was so certain it would be, I repeated the procedure once more, this time getting another old friend to remove another hair strand from the suspect's person. Apparently, he passed her in a public place, and plucked. The strand matched the first one, but didn't belong to Sylvy Sobol.

I didn't warn this woman at all because I didn't feel as if I had put her in danger. If she were suspicious about the hair pulling incident, I felt it was her responsibility to leave town on her own.

The third candidate was on the Moon, in Hadley. I had no trouble finding her, which seemed odd, but she didn't check out either. I returned to Armstrong, both stumped and annoyed.

The logical conclusion was that my DNA sample was false—that it wasn't the sample for Sylvy Sobol. I had taken the sample from the Interstellar DNA database, and there was the possibility that the sample had been changed or tainted. I had heard of such a thing being done, but had always dismissed it as impossible. Those samples were the most heavily guarded in the universe. Even if someone managed to get into the system, they would encounter back-ups upon back-ups, and more encryption than I wanted to think about.

So I contacted Anetka and asked her to send me a DNA sample of her mother. She did, and I ran it against the sample I had. Mine had been accurate. The women I had seen were not Sylvy Sobol.

I had never, in my entire career, made an error of this magnitude. One of those women should have been the former Mrs. Sobol. Unless my information was wrong. Unless I was operating from incorrect assumptions. Still, the assumptions shouldn't have mattered in this search. A pregnant woman wasn't that difficult to hide, not when she was taking transport elsewhere. I'd even found the one who'd remained on Earth.

No. The incorrect assumption had to come after the pregnancy ended. The children. Transport registries always keep track of the sex of the fetus, partly as a response to a series of lawsuits where no one could prove that the woman who claimed she'd lost a fetus on board a transport had actually been pregnant. The transports do not do a DNA check—such things are considered violations of privacy in all but criminal matters—but they do require pregnant women to submit a doctor's report on the health of the mother and the fetus before the woman is allowed to board.

I'd searched out pregnant women, but only those carrying a single daughter. Not twins or multiples. And no males.

Anetka had mentioned failed clones. Clones failed for a variety of reasons, but they only failed in large numbers when someone was using a defective gene or was trying to make a significant change on the genetic level. If the changes didn't work at the genetic level, surgery was performed later to achieve the same result and the DNA remained the same.

I had Anetka's DNA. I'd taken it that first day without her knowing it. I ran client DNA only when I felt I had no other choice; sometimes to check identity, sometimes to check for past crimes. I hadn't run Anetka's—photographic, vid, and those enhancements made it obvious that she was who she said she was. I knew she wasn't concealing her identity, and there was no way she was fronting for a Disty or any other race. She had told me she was a clone. So I felt a DNA check was not only redundant, it was also unnecessary because it didn't give me the kind of information I was searching for.

But now things were different. I needed to check it to see if she was a repaired child, if there had been some flaw in the fetus that couldn't have been altered in the womb. I hadn't looked for repaired children when I'd done the hospital records scans. I hadn't looked for anything that complicated at all.

So I ran the DNA scan. It only took a second, and the results were not what I expected.

Anetka Sobol wasn't a repaired child, at least not in the sense that I had been looking for. Anetka Sobol was an altered child.

According to her DNA, Anetka Sobol had once been male.

9

IF THE TRAIL hadn't been so easy to follow once I realized I was looking for a woman pregnant with a boy, I wouldn't have traced it. I would have gone immediately to Anetka and called her on it. But the trail was easy to follow, and any one of my competitors would have done so—perhaps earlier because they had different methods than I did. I knew at least three of them that ran DNA scans on clients as a matter of course.

If Anetka went to any of them after I refused to complete the work, they would find her mother. It would take them three days. It took me less, but that was because I was better.

10

Sylvy Sobol ran a small private university in the Gagarin Dome on the Moon. She went by the name Celia Walker, and she had transferred from a school out past the Disty homeworld where she had spent the first ten years of her exile. She had run the university for fifteen years.

Gagarin had been established fifty years after Armstrong, and was run by a governing board, the only colony that had such a government. The board placed covenants on any person who owned or rented property within the interior of the dome. The covenants covered everything from the important, such as oxygen regulators, to the unimportant, such as a maintenance schedule for each building, whether the place needed work or not. Gagarin did not tolerate any rules violations. If someone committed three such violations—whether they be failing to follow the maintenance schedule or murder—that person was banned from the dome for life.

The end result was that residents of Gagarin were quiet, law-abiding, and suspicious. They watched me as if I were a particularly distasteful bug when I got off the high speed train from Armstrong. I learned later that I didn't meet the dome's strict dress code.

I had changed into something more appropriate after I got my hotel room, and then went to the campus. The university was a technical school for undergraduates, most of them local, but a few came in from other parts of the Moon. The administrative offices were in a low building with fake adobe facades. The classrooms were in some of Gagarin's only high rises, and were off limits to visitors.

I didn't care about that. I went straight to the Chancellor's office, and buzzed myself in, even though I didn't have an appointment. Apparently, the open campus policy that the on-line brochures proudly proclaimed extended to the administrative offices as well.

Sylvy Sobol sat behind a desk made of Moon clay. Ancient southwestern tapestries covered the walls, and matching rugs covered the floor. The permaplastic here had been covered with more fake adobe, and the net effect was to make this seem like the American Southwest hundreds of years before.

She looked no different than the age-enhancement programs on my computer led me to believe she'd look. Her dark hair was laced with silver, her eyes had laugh lines in the corners, and she was as slender as she had been when she disappeared. She wore a blouse made of the same weave as the tapestries, and a pair of tan cargo pants. Beneath the right sleeve of her blouse a stylish wrist-top glistened. When she saw me, she smiled. "May I help you?"

I closed the door, walked to her desk, and showed her my license. Her eyes widened ever so slightly, and then she covered the look.

"I came to warn you," I said.

"Warn me?" She straightened almost imperceptibly, but managed to look perplexed. Behind the tightness of her lips, I sensed fear.

"You and your son need to use a new service, and disappear again. It's not safe for you anymore."

"I'm sorry, Mr.—Flint?—but I'm not following you."

"I can repeat what I said, or we can go somewhere where you'd feel more comfortable talking."

She shook her head once, then stood. "I'm not sure I know what we'd be talking about."

I reached out my hand. I had my palm scanner in it. Anyone who'd traveled a lot, anyone who had been on the run, would recognize it. "We can do this the old-fashioned way, Mrs. Sobol, or you can listen to me."

She sat down slowly. Her lower lip trembled. She didn't object to my use of her real name. "If you're what your identification says you are, you don't warn people. You take them in."

I let my hand drop. "I was hired by Anetka Sobol," I said. "She wanted me to find you. She claimed that she wanted to share her inheritance with her Original. She's a clone. The record supports this claim."

"So, you want to take us back." Her voice was calm, but her eyes weren't. I watched her hands. They remained on the desktop, flat, and she was without enhancement. So far, she hadn't signaled anyone for help.

"Normally, I would have taken you back. But when I discovered that Anetka's Original was male, I got confused."

Sylvy licked her lower lip, just like her cloned daughter did. A hereditary nervous trait.

I rested one leg on the corner of the desk. "Why would a man change the sex of a clone when the sex didn't matter? Especially if all he wanted was the child. A man with no violent tendencies, who stood accused of attacking his wife so savagely all she could do was leave him, all she could do was disappear. Why would he do that?"

She hadn't moved. She was watching me closely. Beads of perspiration had formed on her upper lip.

"So I went back through the records and found two curious things. You disappeared just after his business on Korsve failed. And once you moved to Gagarin, you and your son were often in other domed Moon colonies at the same time as your husband. Not a good way to hide from someone, now is it, Mrs. Sobol?"

She didn't respond.

I picked up a clay pot. It was small and very, very old. It was clearly an original, not a Moon-made copy. "And then there's the fact that your husband never bothered to change his will to favor the child he had raised. It wouldn't have mattered to most parents that the child was a clone, especially when the Original was long gone. He could have arranged a dispensation, and then made certain that the business remained in family hands." I set the pot down. "But he had already done that, hadn't he? He hoped that the Wygnin would forget."

She made a soft sound in the back of her throat, and backed away from me, clutching at her wrist. I reached across the desk and grabbed her left arm, keeping her hand away from her wrist-top. I wasn't ready for her to order someone to come in here. I still needed to talk to her alone.

"I'm not going to turn you in to the Wygnin," I said. "I'm not going to let anyone know where you are. But if you don't listen to me, someone else will find you, and soon."

She stared at me, the color high in her cheeks. Her arm was rigid beneath my hand.

"The will was your husband's only mistake," I said. "The Wygnin never forget. They targeted your firstborn, didn't they? The plants on Korsve didn't open and close without a fuss. Something else happened. The Wygnin only target firstborns for a crime that can't be undone."

She shook her arm free of me. She rubbed the spot where my hand had touched her flesh, then she sighed. She seemed to know I wouldn't go away. When she spoke, her voice was soft. "No Wygnin were on the site planning committee. We bought the land, and built the plants according to our customs. At that point, the Wygnin didn't understand the concept of land purchase."

I noted the use of the word "we." She had been involved with the Third Dynasty, more involved than the records said.

"We built on a haven for nestlings. You understand nestlings?"

"I thought they were a food source."

She shook her head. "They're more than that. They're part of Wygnin society in a way we didn't understand.

They become food only after they die. It's the shells that are eaten, not the nestlings themselves. The nestlings themselves are considered sentient."

I felt myself grow cold. "How many were killed?"

She shrugged. "The entire patch. No one knows for sure. We were told, when the Wygnin came to us, that they were letting us off easily by taking our firstborn—Carson's and mine. They could easily take all the children of anyone who was connected with the project, but they didn't."

They could have too. It was the Third Dynasty that acted without regard to local custom, which made it liable to local laws. Over the years, no interstellar court had overturned a ruling in instances like that.

"Carson agreed to it," she said. "He agreed so no one else would suffer. Then we got me out."

"And no one came looking for you until I did."

"That's right," she said.

"I don't think Anetka's going to stop," I said. "I suspect she wants her father to change the will—"

"What?" Sylvy clenched her collar with her right hand, revealing the wrist-top. It was one of the most sophisticated I'd seen.

"Anetka wants control of the Third Dynasty, and I was wondering why her father hadn't done a will favoring her. Now I know. She was probably hoping I couldn't find you so that her father would change the will in her favor."

"He can't," Sylvy said.

"I'm sure he might consider it, if your son's life is at stake," I said. "The Wygnin treat their captives like family—

indeed, make them into family, but the techniques they use on adults of other species are—"

"No," she said. "It's too late for Carson to change his will."

She was frowning at me as if I didn't understand anything. And it took me a moment to realize how I'd been used.

Anetka Sobol had tricked me in more ways than I cared to think about. I wasn't half as good as I thought I was. I felt the beginnings of an anger I didn't need. I suppressed it. "He's dead, isn't he?"

Sylvy nodded. "He died three years ago. He installed a personal alarm that notified me the moment his heart stopped. My son has been voting his shares through a proxy program my husband set up during one of his trips here."

I glanced at the wrist-top. No wonder it was so sophisticated. Too sophisticated for a simple administrator. Carson Sobol had given it to her, and through it, had notified her of his death. Had it broken her heart? I couldn't tell, not from three years distance.

She caught me staring at it, and brought her arm down. I turned away, taking a deep breath as the reality of my situation hit me. Anetka Sobol had out-maneuvered me. She had put me in precisely the kind of case I never wanted.

I was working for the Tracker. I was leading a Disappeared to her death and probably the death of her son. "I don't get it," I said. "If something happens to your son, Anetka still won't inherit."

Sylvy's smile was small. "She inherits by default. My son will disappear, and stop voting the proxy program. She'll set up a new proxy program and continue to vote the shares. I'm sure the Board thinks she's the person behind the votes anyway. No one knows about our son."

"Except for you, and me, and the Wygnin." I closed my eyes. "Anetka had no idea you'd had a son."

"No one did," Sylvy said. "Until now."

I rubbed my nose with my thumb and forefinger. Anetka was good. She had discovered that I was the best and the quickest Retrieval Artist in the business. She had studied me and had known how to reach me. She had also known how to play at being an innocent, how to use my past history to her advantage. She hired me to find her Original, and once I did, she planned to get rid of him. It would have been easy for her too; no hit man, no attempt at killing. She wouldn't have had to do anything except somehow—surreptitiously—let the Wygnin know how to find the Original. They would have taken him in payment for the Third Dynasty's crimes, he would have stopped voting his shares, and she would have controlled the corporation.

Stopping Anetka wasn't going to be easy. Even if I refused to report, even if Sylvy and her son returned to hiding, Anetka would continue looking for them.

I had doomed them. If I left this case now, I ensured that one of my colleagues would take it. They would find Sylvy and her son. My colleagues weren't as good as I was, but they were good. And they were smart enough to follow the bits of my trail that I couldn't erase.

The only solution was to get rid of Anetka. I couldn't kill her. But I could think of one other way to stop her.

I opened my eyes. "If I could get Anetka out of the business, and allow you and your son to return home, would you do so?"

Sylvy shook her head. "This is my home," she said. She glanced at the fake adobe walls, the southwestern decor. Her fingers touched a blanket hanging on the wall beside her. "But I can't answer for my son."

"If he doesn't do anything, he'll be running for the rest of his life."

She nodded. "I still can't answer for him. He's an adult now. He makes his own choices."

As we all did.

"Think about it," I said, handing her a card with my chip on it. "I'll be here for two days."

11

THEY HIRED ME, of course. What thinking person wouldn't? I had to guarantee that I wouldn't kill Anetka when I got her out of the business—and I did that, by assuring Sylvy that I wasn't now nor would I ever be an assassin—and I had to guarantee that I would get the Wygnin off her son's trail.

I agreed to both conditions, and for the first time in years, I did something other than tracking a Disappeared.

Through channels, I let it drop that I was searching for the real heir to Carson Sobol's considerable fortune. Then I showed some of my actual research—into the daughter's history, the falsified birth date, the inaccurate records. I managed to dump information about Anetka's cloning and her sex change, and I tampered with the records to show that her clone mark had been faked just as her sex had. Alterations, done at birth, made her look like a clone when she really wasn't.

I made sure that my own work on-line looked like sloppy detecting, but I hid the changes I made in other files. I did all of this quickly and thoroughly, and by the time I was done, it appeared as though Carson Sobol had hidden his own heir—originally a son—by making him into a daughter and passing him off as a clone.

At that point, I could have sat back and let events move forward by themselves. But I didn't. This had become personal.

I had to see Anetka one last time.

I set an appointment to hand deliver my final bill.

12

THIS TIME she was wearing emeralds, an entire sheath covered with them. I had heard that there would be a gala event honoring one of the galaxy's leaders, but I had forgotten that the event would be held in Armstrong, at one of the poshest restaurants on the Moon.

She was sweeping up her long hair, letting it fall just below the mark on the back of her head, when I entered. As she turned, she stabbed an emerald hair comb into the bun at the base of her neck.

"I don't have much time," she said.

"I know." I closed the door. "I wanted give you my final bill."

"You found my sister?" There was a barely concealed excitement in her voice.

"No." The room smelled of an illegal perfume. I was surprised no one had confiscated it when she got off the shuttle and then I realized she probably hadn't taken a shuttle. Even the personal items bag she wore that first day had been part of her act. "I'm resigning."

She shook her head slightly. "I might have known you would. You have enough money now, so you're going to quit."

"I have enough information now to know you're not the kind of person I relish working for."

She raised her eyebrows. The movement dislodged the tiny emerald attached to her left cheek. She caught it just before it fell to the floor. "I thought you were done investigating me."

"Your father's dead," I said. "He has been for three years, although the Third Dynasty has managed to keep that information secret, knowing the effect his death would have had on galactic confidence in the business."

She stared at me for a moment, clearly surprised. "Only five of us knew that."

"Six," I said.

"You found my mother." She stuck the emerald in its spot.

"You found the alarm. You knew she'd been notified of your father's death."

The emerald wasn't staying on her cheek. Anetka let out a puff of air, then set the entire kit down. "I really didn't appreciate the proxy program," she said. "It notified me of my insignificance an hour after my father breathed his last. It told me to go about my life with my own fortune and abandon my place in the Third Dynasty to my Original."

"Which you didn't do."

"Why should I? I knew more about the business than she ever would."

"Including the Wygnin."

She leaned against the dressing table. "You're much better than I thought."

"And you're a lot more devious than I gave you credit for."

She smiled and tapped her left cheek. "It's the face. Youth still fools."

Perhaps it did. I usually didn't fall for it, though. I couldn't believe I had this time. I had simply thought I was being as cautious as usual. What Anetka Sobol had taught me was that being as cautious as usual wasn't cautious enough.

"Pay me, and I'll get out of here," I said.

"You've found my mother. You may as well tell me where she is."

"So you can turn your Original over to the Wygnin?"

That flat look came back into her eyes. "I wouldn't do that."

"How would you prevent it? The Wygnin have a valid debt."

"It's twenty-seven years old."

"The Wygnin hold onto markers for generations." I paused, then added, "As you well know."

"You can't prove what I do and do not know."

I nodded. "True enough. Information is always tricky. It's so easy to tamper with."

Her eyes narrowed. She was smart, probably one of the smartest people I'd ever come up against. She knew I was referring to something besides our discussion.

"So I'm getting out." I handed her a paper copy of the bill—rare, unnecessary, and expensive. She knew that as well as I did. Then, as soon as she took the paper from my hand, I pressed my wrist-top to send the electronic version. "You owe me money. I expect payment within the hour."

She crumpled the bill. "You'll get it."

"Good." I pulled open the door.

"You know," she said, just loud enough for me to hear, "if you can find my mother, anyone can."

"I've already thought of that," I said, and left.

13

THE WYGNIN CAME for her later that night, toward the end of the gala. Security tried to stop them until they showed a valid warrant for the heir of Carson Sobol. The entire transaction caused an interstellar incident, and the vidnets were filled with it for days. The Third Dynasty used its attorneys to try to prove that Anetka was the eighth clone, just as everyone thought she was, but the Wygnin didn't believe it.

The beautiful thing about a clone is that it is a human being. It's simply one whose heritage matches another person's exactly, and whose facts of birth are odder than most. These are facts, yes, but they are facts that can be explained in other ways. The Wygnin simply chose to believe my explanations, not Anetka's. It was the sex change that did it. The Wygnin believed that anyone who would change a child's sex to protect it would also brand it with a clone mark, even if the mark wasn't accurate.

Over time, the lawyers lost all of their appeals, and Anetka disappeared into the Wygnin culture, never to be heard from again.

Oh, of course, the Third Dynasty still believes it's being run by Anetka Sobol voting her shares, as she always has, through a proxy program. Her Original apparently decided not to return to claim his prize. He acts as he always planned to, secretly. Only Sylvy Sobol, her son, and I know the person voting those shares isn't Anetka.

After Anetka's future was sealed, I stopped paying attention to the business of the Third Dynasty. I still don't look. I don't want to know if I have traded one monster for another. Some cold-heartedness is trained—and I can make myself think that Carson Sobol never once treated young Anetka with love, affection, or anything bordering civility—but I am smart enough to know that most cold-heartedness is bred into the genes. Just because Anetka is gone, doesn't mean the Original won't act the same way in similar circumstances.

And what is my excuse for my cold-heartedness? I'd like to say I've never done anything like this before, but I have—always in the name of my client, or a Disappeared. This time, though, this time, I did it for me.

Anetka Sobol had out-thought me, had compromised me, and had made me do the kind of work I'd vowed I'd never do. I let a front use me to open a door that would allow other Trackers to find a Disappeared.

People disappear because they want to. They disappear to escape a bad life, or a mistake they've made, or they disappear to save themselves from a horrible death. A person who has disappeared never wants to be found.

I always ignored that simple fact, thinking I knew better. But one man is never a good judge of another, even if he thinks he is.

I tell myself Anetka Sobol would have destroyed her Original if she had had the chance. I tell myself Anetka Sobol was greedy and self-centered. I tell myself Anetka Sobol deserved her fate.

But I can't ignore the fact that when I learned that Anetka Sobol had used me, this case became personal, in a way I would never have expected. Maybe, just maybe, I might have found a different solution, if she hadn't angered me so.

And now she haunts me in the middle of the night. She wakes me out of many a sound sleep. She keeps me restless and questioning. Because I didn't go after her for who she was or what she was planning. I had worked with people far worse than she was. I had met others who had done horrible things, things that made me wonder if they were even human. Anetka Sobol wasn't in their league.

No. I had gone after her for what she had done to me. For what she had made me see about myself. And because I hadn't liked my reflection in the mirror she held up, I destroyed her.

I can't get her back. No one comes back intact from the Wygnin. She will spend the rest of her days there. And I will spend the rest of mine thinking about her.

Some would say that is justice. But I have come to realize, in a universe as complex as this one, justice no longer exists.

About the Author

International bestselling writer Kristine Kathryn Rusch has won two Hugo awards, a World Fantasy Award, and six *Asimov's* Readers Choice Awards. She writes mystery as Kris Nelscott, romance as Kristine Grayson, Kristine Dexter, and Kris DeLake, and sf and fantasy as Kristine Kathryn Rusch. For more information about her work, please go to kristinekathrynrusch.com.

Also by
Kristine Kathryn Rusch

The Retrieval Artist Series:

The Disappeared
Extremes
Consequences
Buried Deep
Paloma
Recovery Man
Duplicate Effort
Anniversary Day
Blowback

The Smokey Dalton Series (as Kris Nelscott):

A Dangerous Road
Smoke-Filled Rooms
Thin Walls
Stone Cribs
War at Home
Days of Rage